THINGS I PRAY I NEVER FORGET

A Collection of Stories

Doug S. Haines

Some of the stories in this collection have appeared or are scheduled to appear elsewhere: "The Experiment" in *Slippery Elm*, "The Solicitation of Tom W" in *Down in the Dirt Magazine*, "Limited Space" in *Drunk Monkeys*, "Buzzards" in *West Trade Review*, "The Barrelman" in *Reed Magazine,* and "Meat" in *The Chicago Tribune's Printers Row*. In addition, I wish to thank Tim Johnston, Courtney Miller Santo, Cary Holladay, Christopher J. Oglesby, Scott Kaukonen, Mark Wisniewski, and the late Paul Ruffin for their continued support and writerly wisdom through the years.

Published by Unsolicited Press
www.unsolicitedpress.com

Unsolicited Press Books are distributed to the trade by Ingram.
ISBN: 978-1-947021-19-8
Cover Design: In-house UP team

Attention schools and businesses. Discount copies are available for bulk orders. Please contact our team at info@unsolicitedpress.com.

To my mother. You are missed.

TABLE OF CONTENTS

LIMITED SPACE

Walter Bumpus was forty-three days shy of his eighty-first birthday when his calendar finally ran out. His last words were less than poetic.

"Not too shabby," he said, placing his empty dish on the counter. "I think I'll have that again for dinner. Leave it out and I'll fix another plate when I get hungry," he told wife number three, as he shuffled across the linoleum floor stabbing the tile with his cane for traction and stability. His wife nodded in faint recognition of her husband's declaration and went on violently scrubbing a casserole dish over the sink as if it had done her harm in a past life. Theirs was a relationship built on good housekeeping and very few words.

Dora had been the Bumpus family's maid for more than thirty years and only married Walter twelve years prior after wife number two lost her bout with cancer. Dora continued to look after Walter, and he included her in his will. That was the deal. He knew Dora had never had a retirement plan before and that she found great comfort in this arrangement because Walter had a green thumb when it came to growing dollar bills. He joked in front of his friends that Dora was sharing a bed with her 401k.

"Mr. Walt is nice enough and much too old to get frisky, so it's not so bad," she often joked in her defense. "He provides good. Besides, he always make me laugh."

***

In 1953, Walter Bumpus opened Bumpus Pawn with his older brother Harold. Seven years later, he bought Harold out and became the sole proprietor. The business flourished under Walter's personable demeanor and keen eye for a deal. He was a world class haggler and could whittle down the financial dreams of the poor and desperate with the best of them. He felt no guilt or shame. It was business—nothing personal.

Earlier that morning at precisely 7 a.m., Walter arrived at the shop, struggled to park and exit his '65 Lincoln Continental, and waddled to the door where he fumbled through his keys until finding the right one to start the day. He'd been doing the same thing every single day, except for Sundays, for as long as he could remember, and it never dawned on him that today might be his last.

When the key finally tripped the mechanism, Walter entered with his usual lumbering stagger, shutting the door behind him, and made his way to the alarm system. The sound grated on him as he strained to see the tiny numbers on the keypad and defuse the blaring noise. It reminded him of the war-—not the sound, but rather the tension it created inside him. He took a deep breath once it had ceased and settled into his usual spot behind the old pine-top desk. Hidden among the file cabinets was a small dorm fridge containing what remained of the previous day's thirty-pack of Miller High Life. He took one out, wiped off the lid, opened it, and carefully poured its contents into a coffee mug that bore a picture of a dog that had been dead for over a decade. He'd loved that dog.

He sat in the dark sipping from his mug for the next thirty or forty minutes until Lyndle arrived with his own coffee mug full of beer. Lyndle Wells was a middle-aged honky-tonk musician and Texas outlaw who worked part time at the shop to pay back his various loan tickets. Walter enjoyed his company and valued their friendship, and even saw Lyndle as the son he'd never had. Of course, Walter would never tell him any of this. A thing like that might go to the boy's head. They spent the next few hours chatting about politics and the crosswords and pausing, occasionally, to sip from their mugs. In these moments, Walter felt closer to Lyndle than anyone else in the world.

At around 10:30 a.m., the store got its first customer of the day. It was a skinny nervous kid with an old Rickenbacker he was eager to sell—almost too eager. Walter's first assumption was that the guitar was stolen, but after talking with the boy he decided that the deal appeared to be on the up and up.

"So, you've decided to go a cappella?" he joked.

Lyndle gave the old man a slight courtesy laugh, most likely wondering how many times he'd heard Walter tell that same joke. After a few minutes of haggling, Walter conned the poor boy out of the guitar for a few hundred dollars. He'd be sure to turn a profit on it, if only he had the time to do so. Meanwhile, Lyndle found a place in the window for the shop's newest treasure and set it out on display. The guitar's cherry red sunburst shimmered like an angel from a dream. In a few hours the sun would reflect perfectly off it and temporarily blind anyone who crossed its path as it called out to be played.

That was about all the action the store saw that morning, with the exception of a moderately priced accordion Lyndle managed to sell to a young Mexican woman who had excessively high hopes of Tejano stardom for her unsuspecting fourteen-year-old son. There'd also been a couple of well-dressed Mormons who stopped by on their mountain bikes to peddle their version of God to the two men sipping High Life from their coffee mugs.

"Son, you're wasting your breath," the old man said, refusing to accept the boys' copy of *The Book of Mormon.* Walter was raised Baptist but had recently started accompanying Dora to the Sunday Mass at St. Michael's on Third. He didn't really know what he believed but found some comfort in the concept of God, figuring it had to be better than the alternative. Still, he was naturally suspicious of all religions and especially of anyone trying to sell him on one.

"But, sir, don't you care about salvation—about a better life?" the blonder of the two boys asked.

"I think it's a little late for that, son. Let's just say the milk is already startin' to smell funny."

The boys looked at each other. The fluorescent lights of the shop seemed to echo off their straw-like hair as they exchanged looks of bewilderment.

"He's pretty well past his expiration date, ya dig?" Lyndle added to clear up the confusion.

"But that's all the more reason to open your heart, sir. We've felt the spirit, and it's our mission to bear our testimony and show others the light. The Kingdom of Heaven is—"

"Crowded?" Walter stood up from behind the desk and began to approach the boys. "At least, that's what I hear. I know all about how y'all think there's some kind of limited space in Heaven, and how it's reserved only for *your* chosen few. And if that's the case, then why the hell are you here trying to recruit me? If there's limited space in Heaven and I knew about it, I'd be keeping the key to salvation all to myself—not telling a soul."

"But, sir, that's not—"

"No shit, Walt!" Lyndle snorted. "Can you imagine wasting your whole life trying to be good and righteous only to walk through the Pearly Gates and find out the place is packed asshole-to-bellybutton with blond headed kids on bicycles wearin' their starched white shirts and clip-on ties? Man, that'd be the cruelest joke of all."

The boys were becoming agitated. "Sirs, it's not like that. You're thinking of the Jehovah's Witnesses. We're—"

"Look, son, it seems to me you kids have gotten yourselves all tied up in some sort of pyramid scheme here. And I know it's not your fault. You were born into this, but that's no reason to go around preaching something that was read out of a hat. The whole thing is science fiction, if you ask me. Now I've got work to do, so you boys best move it along and sell your version of Jesus elsewhere, 'cause we ain't buying." Walter worked his cane like a cattle prod as he ushered the two young men out the door of the shop.

"Wally, I think you might be confusing The Church of Latter-day Saints with that crazy Scientology shit them movie stars are all into," Lyndle said once the missionaries were safely out of earshot.

"Nah, I know the difference."

"And what's that?"

"The difference *is* there ain't no difference. Scientologists are nothin' more than fancy space Mormons, that's all. It's all based on hierarchy and recruitment. Those at the top prosper and those at the bottom do all the work. They might as well be selling knives door-to-door instead of God or salvation. That's the problem with all religions."

"And why's *that* a problem?" Lyndle asked.

"People, by nature, are greedy. They all want more—more power—more money—more of God's sweet blessings and this corrupts'm completely. It's the same reason socialism continually fails and the pawn business is always booming. People want more than they can afford. Personally, I don't know how God puts up with it, but it's certainly kept food on my table the last fifty some-odd years."

"And how does that have anything to do with what we were just talking about?" Lyndle grinned.

The old man did not return the smile. He could tell Lyndle was just trying to get his goat, and he had had enough. "Ah, you can go to hell for all I care, Lyndle Wells, 'cause I'm going to lunch. Keep an eye on the shop and don't go borrowing anything." Walter gathered his things and began making his way towards the door. "Especially that Rickenbacker," he barked over his shoulder.

"All right, but you gotta pick up another thirty pack on your way back. This one is about done-fer." Lyndle opened the second to last beer in the fridge and leaned dangerously back in his chair. There was a slight crackle in the wood and a momentary battle for balance before Lyndle regained his cool.

The old man smiled at this and shook his head. "Well, we'll just call you *Grace* from now on."

"I don't care what you call me, just don't forget the beer. I'll pay ya back."

"I'm old—not senile or stupid, Lynn."

"Coulda fooled me."

"You keep talkin', boy, and I'll come swat you outta your roost and have me a big ol' laugh when you bust your ass."

"Well, maybe you could pick yourself up some wine coolers and some of that Mormon literature you seem to like so much. You know, to brighten your perspective."

"My perspective will be plenty bright the day you start buying the beer 'round here, Mr. Wells."

"That hurts, Walt."

"Truth always does, *Grace*."

Walter let the door swing shut behind him as he teetered slowly towards the factory blue Lincoln that had spent the morning baking in the West Texas sun. The suicide doors were opened to allow the heat to escape quickly while accepting the old man's briefcase and cane into the rear of the vehicle. Walt wiped his forehead with a blood-stained monogrammed handkerchief that had been a gift from wife number one on a birthday too far in the past to recall. He eased himself down into the driver's seat and positioned himself behind the wheel. The engine roared with American pride. The car was handling its age far better than the driver. The Lincoln would be around for a long time to come.

***

After lunch that afternoon, Walter took his dessert on the porch swing. It creaked under his weight as he rocked back and forth. The breeze was cool in the shade and the pecan pie was rich. His mind wandered for a few minutes. He thought about two dead wives, a couple of good dogs, the Baptists of his youth, Lyndle's hell raising, Dora's Catholicism, and the blond boys with their mountain bikes and clip-on ties and limited space. Could Saint Peter really be *that* picky? And if he was, then wasn't it all a crapshoot, one religion versus another? How could anyone know? It was like picking a horse at the races. All anyone can really do is just look at the stats sheet and weigh the odds. All bets are placed with faith.

Before dozing off for a short spell, Walt pictured a blue-eyed Jesus on the cross. He looked young but weathered. His crow's feet reminded him of Lyndle, and so did his smile. Nailed at the wrists with just enough room to give, the Savior's right hand seemed to beckon the old man forward. When Walt awoke a half hour later, he returned his plate to the kitchen, informed his wife of his dinner plans, and sluggishly disappeared down the hall. Lyndle Wells would have to buy his own beer from now on.

Dora's 401k cashed out.

The ad in the paper the following week was simple and to the point:

Clearance Sale at Bumpus Pawn—Prices Slashed—Everything Must Go!

BUZZARDS

Slightly wine-drunk and flying down some unfamiliar back road in a late '90s minivan with a 22-year-old kid she'd pretty much just met behind the wheel, Abigail Wilson, a junior partner in her now ex-husband's law firm, tried to convince herself that she was up for anything. She knew her friends would call this *dangerous behavior*, but she also couldn't remember the last time she'd had this much fun. She was smiling and laughing—actually laughing, from the belly up. Daryl hadn't made her laugh in years. In fact, she couldn't remember the last time he'd made her laugh, really laugh. Had he ever?

Of course, this was definitely not her idea of a normal first date, but then again Abigail had been out of the game for a long time—too long. And she had to admit that she'd had fun all afternoon. It was one of those rare perfect Texas days in late September where it's warm and breezy, as opposed to hot and muggy. She looked at her date. His forearms were muscular and painted like a mural. She'd met him in the coffee shop near the office, and he had always served her vanilla lattes with a side of flirtation. He was cute in that rugged, tatted, Austin musician kind of way. He was also far too young for a woman her age. This she knew. At least that's what she told herself the first four times he'd flirted with her. But this last time was different. Her resistance was swayed by the surprisingly powerful combination of his blue eyes, his Paul Newman-like smile, and her current string of bad luck and low self-esteem. And now here she was.

The radio blasted Otis Redding and she sang along while the cute boy behind the wheel smiled smugly. She got the feeling he had already chalked her up to his list of conquests, and she didn't care. She didn't care that he was covered in tatts or far too young for her. She didn't care that he worked in a coffee shop for minimum wage so he could pay the rent until his band *made it*. She didn't care about any of it. She just wanted to have fun. That was all.

He'd told her he was taking her to some spot he knew of off the Pedernales to "watch the sunset" and drink more wine, but the sun was the last thing on her mind as it hung in orange limbo on the horizon. A Scooby Doo air freshener and a set of graduation tassels spun around beneath the rearview mirror, and she thought for a moment that this was all a huge mistake. He probably took all the desperate and lonely *cougars* or *MILFs* or whatever they're calling grown women these days to this "special spot," and then she stopped herself. That was *old Abigail* talking, and she's no fun. Sometimes a woman needs to let loose, doesn't she?

The facts were simple. Her career was as good as dead as long as she stayed at Kaufman, Wilson, and Pennington. Daryl would certainly see to that. And this mixture of Otis, red wine, the cute and flirty tatted barista, and an eight-month dry spell was beginning to work its magic. Maybe this boy was really her conquest and not the other way around. When she looked at life this way, it didn't seem so dangerous. Instead, it seemed almost primal. Almost necessary for her sanity's survival. Abigail Wilson then decided to dismiss her concerns and allow her inhibitions to disappear faster than the sun ever could. This barista could be exactly what she needed.

"You're very beautiful," he shouted over her singing.

She felt her cheeks grow flushed and smiled.

"But you can't sing for shit, Abby."

She laughed because he was right and because she liked it when he called her *Abby*. *Abigail* had begun to feel like an old lady's name, a spinster, the type that lives alone in a forgotten house at the end of the street with her fourteen cats running amuck as the empty tuna cans pile up around her. A girl named *Abby* sounded like she had her entire life ahead of her—like she'd never been divorced or even married—like the years she'd wasted on Daryl didn't even exist. She reached over to turn down the volume, and Otis faded to a murmur as she spoke.

"I'm so glad you talked me into this."

"I didn't talk you into anything. You always wanted to go."

Cocky little shit, she thought, but decided to ignore it. She reminded herself that she deserved this. She deserved a fling. Everybody else was doing it. Daryl certainly did. She looked at the boy and he grinned. The car slowed almost to a stop, and he turned left and began to ease down a gravel road.

"I think we're safe to open up one of the bottles," he said.

"I like the way you think, baby." Her sultry voice was so out of character, so not Abigail. And *baby*, really? She felt like Mrs. Robinson, but she couldn't help herself. She struggled with the corkscrew on the rough road, but eventually popped the cork and took a large swig straight from the bottle. Classy. If only Daryl could see her now. This thought made her both happy and sad. She often felt this way when nostalgia crept in. She looked over at the boy and caught him stealing a glance at her freshly shaved legs. The sundress she'd chosen for this adventure looked good, she knew it did, but it also felt nice for someone else to notice. All those nights at the gym watching reruns of *Chopped* and *Kitchen Nightmares* while pounding out the preprogramed courses on the elliptical were paying off, and she liked the attention it brought.

He offered her a cigarette from his pack, but she declined. He lit up and a cloud of smoke filled the van. She coughed a little and rolled down her window. He cracked his.

"Which winery is that one from?" he asked.

"The second or the third, I think. I'm pretty sure it's the one I bought from that poor guy that stuttered," she said, and handed him the bottle. She knew exactly which bottle it was—a top-shelf award-winning merlot, as opposed to the cheap table wines he'd purchased on their tour.

With his cigarette in the other hand, he tilted the bottle to his lips, steering the vehicle with one knee. The van veered slightly, but the boy eased it back on track with little effort. He licked his lips and nodded.

"Yep, definitely the expensive shit," he said, and handed the bottle back.

"Can you really taste the difference or are you just patronizing me?"

"Can't it be both?"

"What's that supposed to mean?"

"I don't know, I think you think that I'm too young to know anything about anything, especially wine, but I know a little."

"Really? Like what?"

"I know enough not to spend a hundred bucks on a bottle when a ten dollar one'll get you just as drunk."

"You'll wish you'd spent a little more when that ten-dollar hangover kicks in."

"Hangovers are for pussies."

She didn't care for the tone or the implications of his response and changed the subject.

"So, can you float the Pedernales?"

"Depends, but that's not exactly where we're going and definitely not what we're going to do. I was just using the river as a reference point," he explained.

"Reference points only work if the person you are referring them to knows where they are."

"Are you telling me you've never been to the Pedernales?" he asked, shaking his head. "Next you'll tell me you've never heard of LBJ."

"Elby who?"

"Nice, I forgot you probably voted for him."

"Fuck you."

He put his hands up as if to surrender. "Easy, I was just teasing."

"My parents hadn't even met yet. How fucking old do you think I am?" She glared but it was useless. This boy was not to be taken seriously. He was a child, a hipster barista, a slinger of lattes—nothing more, she told herself. If he wanted to play rough on the age front, she could oblige.

"So, is this your mother's minivan? It's awfully sweet of her to let you borrow it."

"No, it's mine—paid in full."

"And why would a twenty-something-year-old guy want to drive a minivan? It's kind of a grocery grabber, isn't it?"

"Yep, but you soccer moms love it." He took a long drag on his cigarette and smothered it in the ashtray. "Admit it. You got a little tingly down there when you first saw it." He put his hand on her thigh and squeezed.

She shifted in her seat and cleared her throat. He returned his hand to the wheel.

"Do you promise it's not your mother's?"

"Pinky swear," he said, holding up and wiggling his little finger.

"Then, why?"

"Why the grocery grabber?"

"Yeah."

"I bought it for my band."

"Of course you did." She shook her head. "Another fucking musician." She paused for second and looked around the back of the van. "Isn't this a little small for that?"

"We're a small band—just a three-piece. Besides, we've got a trailer and this thing gets pretty good gas mileage on the highway. And what do you mean *another fucking musician?*"

"You're not my first. I went to college here. You can't throw a penny around Austin without hitting a musician and watching him scramble to pick it up."

He drove in silence for a moment. "Did you like me better when I was on the barista track?"

"It's certainly more stable."

"This from the lady that's never been to the Pedernales," he said, steering the conversation back towards their destination and away from his lack of earning potential. "Well, it's a good thing you're pretty." He laughed.

She forced a smile but was starting to see a pattern. Every compliment that came out of his mouth was laced with a deeper insult. She had dated guys like this before and had wasted valuable years of her youth hoping they would change. But with age came experience and wisdom. This boy didn't stand a chance. His mind tricks would only result in the destruction of *his* ego, not hers. Besides, it wasn't like he was a keeper.

Still, there was something about him she liked, and she was determined to enjoy herself no matter what.

When they came to a gate over a cattle guard, he threw the van into park and got out to open the passage. He walked with a swagger that entranced Abigail: arms swinging, head bobbing, legs almost dancing along the dirt road; his lanky frame seemed to ooze confidence as he made his way back to the van.

"So, what's the deal with this place?" she asked when he got back inside the van.

"Back in the eighties, my father and my mom's dad went in on buying this land out here. When my granddad died, he left his half to me, which really pissed my father off, and he sold his half off out of spite as much as profit. It sucks because his half was the half that had the cabin on it."

"What's your half got?"

"A dried out creek bed, a fishing pond that's barely a puddle, and a lot of mesquite and cedar. But from the top of this one rock formation over there," he said, pointing off in the distance, "it's got one hell of a view."

"Is that where we're going?"

"Yep, but we need to hurry. Señor Sol is fading fast."

He drove a little further and then parked the vehicle under an oak. She got out and began to stretch her legs while he rummaged around in the back of the van gathering supplies into an old backpack.

"It's getting a little chilly. Do you have a jacket I can borrow?" she asked, rubbing her shoulders.

"Jesus, what is it about the vagina that makes you people so incapable of handling even the slightest breeze?"

"*You people?*" He had to be kidding, she thought—either that, or he was testing her. "I don't know. What is it about the penis that makes your *people* such assholes?"

"Good question." He smiled and pulled a green hoody from the backpack and tossed it to her. "Will this do?"

"So, I guess you already knew I was going to get cold."

"Well, you are a woman. I just didn't think the complaining was going start this early." He flung the pack over his shoulders and signaled her towards the path.

"For the record, when I start complaining, *you'll* know it."

"Good to know," he said with a shit-eating grin, "but this rock ain't gonna climb itself. Get your sweet ass moving, princess."

"Dick."

"Ah, I like a girl that knows what she wants."

***

He referred to the spot as "The Buzzards' Roost." It was a massive ridge in the middle of nowhere, and Abigail was not dressed for rock climbing. Despite the sweatshirt, her sundress kept blowing over her waist and exposing her pink cotton panties, and her floral print Target flip-flops lacked any traction whatsoever. She slipped once and he caught her, his hand strong and firm against the small of her back.

"I don't think these are the right shoes for this." She giggled, somewhat out of breath.

"You'll be fine. You just have to pay better attention to where you're going." His demeanor was calm in that mocking way of his. Always comforting, always condescending.

"Why don't you lead the way?" she suggested, and he said, "Because I'm enjoying the view too much from back here to take on that kind of responsibility," and this made her smile despite herself. "I bet you are," she said.

He came up behind her and slid his hand around her waist and across her belly, pulling her in close.

She turned her head but avoided his lips, and he kissed her neck instead and nibbled on her ear for a second before releasing her. Then he swatted her on the ass and said, "Giddy up."

***

At the top of the ridge's peak, she had to admit, with the exception of the buzzard shit, the hike was worth it. The view went on forever. He put his arms around her hips and again pulled her close as they watched the sun begin its fade into dusk. He suggested they open another bottle.

"Are you trying to get me drunk?"

"Of course."

Below them and off to her left, she saw the barren creek bed he'd spoken of, and beyond that she saw what was left of the Pedernales River.

"Sad, isn't it? These brutal summers, one right after another, drained all the creeks and rivers." His voice, in its disappointment, was as dry as the land he spoke of.

"Wow, I'm going to call you *half-full*," she said.

"I suppose," he said, without looking at her, "you see the future as all bright and shiny—full of rainbows and unicorns and shit."

Abigail knew more about disappointment and heartache than this boy could ever imagine, but thinking about it made her uncomfortable. She ran her hand along the back of her neck, massaged it, and tried to think of something to say.

"Your problem is that you have no vision," she told him. "When you look at this, you just see a dried out creek bed brought on by drought, and you completely miss the chiseled beauty of the miniature canyon it's evolved into."

He looked puzzled. "You're screwing with me, aren't you?"

"A little bit," she said with her most flirtatious smile.

***

He was a good kisser, soft and passionate. His lips were damp but not wet—certainly not slobbery like some guys. Daryl could learn a thing or two from this kid.

She caught her breath and turned her attention to the question of how they were going to get down in the dark.

"Don't worry about it. I've got you," he told her.

"Okay, you have to stop that."

"Stop what?"

"Maybe I'm just jaded and reading too much into this, but you seem to have a knack for subtly demeaning me. It's misogynistic, and I don't fucking like it."

"Whoa, hold on there, Crazy Train. I had no idea I was doing that. Look, I'm sorry."

"It's okay, just don't do it again," she said.

He looked hurt. "Fine," he said, and sulked off to gather up some kindling in a well-used fire pit full of charred beer cans and wine bottles.

She knew she was not the first to be brought up there and wouldn't be the last.

"I hope you like camping," he said.

"I just wished I'd known ahead of time."

"Would you have come?"

She thought about this for a moment and then shook her head. "Probably not."

"Exactly," he said, and gave her a boyish grin.

Once the fire had been built, Abigail opened two cans of Dinty Moore beef stew and emptied their contents into the blue saucepan and began heating their dinner over the open flame while he pitched the tent. She wanted to give him flack about the tent, about assigning her to woman's work in this outdoor-makeshift kitchen, but the fact was she knew nothing about tents and plenty about heating soup.

"Why can't we just go to the cabin?" she asked.

"I told you. We don't own it anymore."

"We could still sneak over there, couldn't we?"

"Are you trying to get me shot? You do realize that trespassing is a shootable offense, right? Besides, it's got to be a shithole by now. We're better off up here." He looked up at her. "Please don't pout. I'm sorry. But trust me on this."

He cleared the buzzard droppings from a large flat rock with his boot, and they sat down and ate as the last sliver of sun disappeared into the night. After dinner, they continued to drink and talk. He was actually a good listener when he wanted to be. He asked her questions about her life and opinions and general thoughts about the world. His behavior was much improved since she'd scolded him, like a puppy that'd just had his nose rubbed in it. Maybe he was trainable?

"So, what's the absolute most embarrassing moment you've ever had?" he asked. His eyebrows rose with mischief.

She had to think about it. There had been so many embarrassing moments. She wanted to pick something that was more funny than sad, something that had absolutely nothing to do with her ex-husband. This really limited her choices, but then it hit her.

"I once knitted a sweater for a homeless man when I was in college and he didn't like it." The second she said it, she knew she sounded ridiculous.

"You what?"

"You heard me."

"Uh, why?"

"I wanted to do something kind for a fellow human being, and I guess I also wanted to knit something."

They both laughed.

"Is it okay for me to make fun of you now?"

She smiled. "I probably deserve it."

"Knitting, huh? You know my grandmother knits. How old did you say you were? Maybe y'all could hang out."

"I didn't. And I thought we agreed to lay off the age jokes?"

"Fair enough." He paused and regrouped. "So, what kind of sweater was it?"

"I don't know—a sweater."

"Would you describe it as *Cosby* in nature?"

"Yes. Yes, I would. It was very *Cosby* in nature, only without all the roofies and rape. It was earth-toned with horizontal stripes and kind of fuzzy."

"Wow, that's very *Cosby*. And the guy didn't like it? That's shocking."

"Well, I think he was one of those snobby hobos that really just wants the money and not the help."

"I hate those guys."

"Yeah, I guess I do, too."

***

They drank more wine, talked, and made out as the hours slipped away. She liked the attention, and she liked the way he kissed her, but something inside her wouldn't allow things to go any further than a few sloppy kisses and some reckless groping. It wasn't that she didn't want to, because she did, but every time the tension between them became so intense that she felt herself on the verge of losing control, she pulled back, pushing him away. She could tell he was frustrated, and so was she. They'd go back to drinking and talking, and the cycle continued. His patience surprised her.

It was in the middle of one of her better cat stories when Abigail realized her date had passed out on her. It was late, and she decided not to take his disinterest as an insult, and instead helped him to the tent, where she gently guided him down to the sleeping bag. She crawled in with him and tried her best to get comfortable. He spoke nonsense in his sleep. The ground was hard and uneven. Something poked her from underneath. Was this *really* better than the cabin?

After some time, perhaps an hour on the rocky floor of the tent, Abigail finally drifted off, but her sleep was short-lived. She felt the tent rustling and her first thought was *BEAR*. When she opened her eyes, she saw her young companion illuminated by the low hanging full moon outside. She watched for a second as he franticly tried to escape the tent—zipping and unzipping a flap over and over again to no avail.

"What's wrong?" she asked, half asleep.

He muttered something about feeling sick. He did look pale, but it might have been the moonlight.

"I think that's the window, sweetie," she said.

She did her best to redirect him towards the actual door flap, but it was too late. The wine had gotten the best of him. He vomited into the nylon door which acted as a backboard and returned the spray into the tent and onto the two them. Abby moved quickly and used him as a shield before crawling over the boy and making her escape. It was awful and disgusting and embarrassing, but all she could do was laugh. Every decision she'd made that day seemed so absurd. What the hell was she doing with her life? Who was this boy, and why was she really with him?

***

She walked out to the edge of the ridge where they had watched the sunset and he had held her close. The world looked like it went on forever. She thought about the buzzards that called this place home—the scavengers getting by on whatever they found, living on the leftovers the world provided, and picking the bones clean. Such ugly birds, she thought. Ugly but efficient. Survivalists. That's what it's all about, survival. She spread her arms and felt the cool night wind begging her to take flight and finally be free. She heard something and turned around.

Her date stumbled at last out of the tent. He looked pathetic—pale and tragic. He swerved wildly as he walked. He had to be embarrassed, she thought. His steps were awkward and out of sync as he lumbered over to a rock by the fire pit and clumsily took a seat. She smiled. He had been knocked down a few pegs, and she loved it. Control had been passed. Things had changed.

She walked over and put her arm around him, careful to avoid the sick that covered him. She felt almost motherly as she dabbed at the tear that had managed to slip past his remaining pride.

"It's okay," she said. "We'll get you cleaned up."

The boy said something, but his response was unintelligible.

Abigail helped him to his feet and wiped his face with the sleeve of the green hoody he'd given her. She began to laugh again at the ridiculousness of it all, and the sound of her laughter seemed to strike the boy as if he'd been stung by a wasp. He shot up straight and swung his arms wildly as he pulled free and fumbled for his balance.

"You think this is funny?" he said, speaking directly to the fire pit.

She snorted a little, trying not to laugh again, and then gave the boy a playful slap on the ass.

"It's a good thing you're pretty, baby," she said, lightly stroking the side of his face where the tear had been. "'Cause you're a goddamn mess."

He staggered back a few steps and spat vomit from his mouth.

"Don't call me baby, you *old* whore."

In the moonlight, she saw his posture straighten, his back arching and lifting his chest toward the sky. And as he spread his wings, she saw the grin creep slowly across his face.

THE BARRELMAN

The little horse-faced girl looks up at Tuffie McAlister. She has teeth like her mother, minus the one that's missing, and the same pouting blue eyes. She studies him closely as he draws the black border around his bright red mouth. He can feel her watching him. His hand is unsteady and the line is coming out crooked. He sets the paint down and grabs the pill bottle from the table. He rattles it like a maraca, and the girl giggles. Only two Percodan left. A three-week supply gone in one. He has to make a decision, as he stares into the brown plastic container. Take one now, or save'm for the main event? Tuffie looks at the girl and sets the pills down, trading them for the whiskey that sits next to them before putting the finishing touches on his face.

"Why do you have to be a sad clown?" she asks.

"Dunno. Just always have been. It's what people expect." He's not comfortable around children, especially his own. Bad juju and all. "Technically, I'm not a clown, kid. I'm a barrelman. Big difference."

"A bare-what?" she asks.

"A *barrel*-man, Lilly." He shakes his head. "Jesus, didn't your momma teach you anything?"

"What's that?"

"For starters, I'm not funny enough to be a clown." He sets his face paint on the table and surveys his handiwork. There is a cloud of white around his eyes and above each he has drawn in his trademark oversized eyebrows. His tomato-red nose matches his mouth, and there is a small black cross on the tip of his chin that he paints on for luck. He turns to face the girl.

"My job isn't to entertain. My job is to protect. I run interference for the riders and bullfighters. I'm a distraction, that's all." He pulls a flask from his boot, unscrews the cap, drains it, and begins to refill it from the bottle. His hand shakes and the whiskey goes everywhere. He straightens up and tries to focus the pour. Screwing the cap back on, he returns the flask to his boot. "The makeup is tradition—something we do because we've always done it."

"Momma says you're a drunk and that one of these days some bull's gonna give you exactly what you deserve."

"Is that right?" he says. "Well, girl, let me ask you something about your sweet momma. What kind of woman goes off and leaves a goddamn six-year-old at a county fair? I mean, at forty-three, I'm no spring chicken. Hell, I've got broken bones leftover from my bull ridin' days that still ain't healed right. What if I hadn't made the trip? What if I's laid up in some hospital somewhere, or I'd hung up my overalls and face paint a long time ago? Where would you be then? Lost and found? Child services? She didn't know I'd be here. She just left you with that note pinned to your little pink backpack tellin' me *I's* your daddy, fingers crossed I *might* be here." The muscles in his neck are so tight that they feel like they could snap. He rolls his shoulders a couple of times and then begins to massage the pain until it hurts a little more. "This is an awful lot to put on a guy this early in the day," he says under his breath and takes another drink from the bottle. He scratches his head. "I don't get it. I paid my child support—mostly."

"Six and a half," the girl says. She looks like she might cry, but she holds her ground.

"What? Whatever." He catches himself before he says any more. What the hell was that crazy bitch Irene thinking? He's never been the fathering kind. The others were at least smart enough to cash the checks when they came and keep the kids away from the likes of him. Now it looks like he's stuck with one. "Hey, kid, do your old man a favor and grab me that hat and wig off that mannequin over there. I'll be ready in a minute."

"Then you'll take me to see the animals."

"Yeah, then I'll take you." He turns back toward the mirror and whispers, "Yee-freakin'-haw." Both his shoulder and elbow pop as he reaches for his pills and stuffs them into his pocket.

***

She holds onto one of the red bandanas hanging from his loose-fitting size 56 overalls. He is a small man, which helps in the barrel, and the faded denim swallows him and his skinny legs whole. He shows her the pigs and the chickens and the sheep and the goats as they make their way through the livestock show in the pavilion, but all she seems to care about are the ponies. Ponies this and ponies that. What is it with little girls and ponies?

"It smells gross in here," she says.

"Yeah, that's part of it."

"Can I pet the ponies?"

"I don't see why not. In fact, I bet you can ride one if you want to."

She smiles but doesn't say a word.

Inside the *Pony Pen*, she lights up like it's Christmas morning. She releases her grip on the bandana and sprints toward a purebred Welsh. There is a hand painted sign above the stall that reads *Peppermint.* Tuffie tries to follow, but his knees aren't what they used to be. He gives up and lets her go, slowing to a steady hobble. The girl stops just shy of the makeshift corral and stares at the animal, her mouth wide open. The old nag doesn't even bother to look up from her oats. When Tuffie gets there, he steadies himself on the top rail of the corral, looks around to see if anyone is watching, and then kneels down to take a knee and sneak a drink from his boot.

"Looks like you've already got yourself a healthy dose of fear for the beast. That's a good thing."

"Healthy?" she asks.

"That's right, healthy. Fear is a good for you. Don't let anyone ever tell you otherwise." Besides the warmth of the whiskey, Tuffie's stomach is so empty that it feels like it might eat itself. He takes another pull from the flask and finishes it off before returning it to his boot. He'll have to swing by the dressing room before the show. Slowly, he gets to his feet.

"I'm not scared. He's just so pretty is all."

Tuffie leans over, bracing his back with one hand, and takes a look at the horse's undercarriage. "I think he's a she, darlin'."

"*She's* beautiful."

"Ever ride one?"

"No. I've just seen pictures."

"Well, shit. You wanna?"

Her blue eyes widen. "Can I?"

Not one for formality or rules or any kind of procedure or sense of order, Tuffie sweeps the girl up in his arms and places her atop the mare. The animal is startled. It turns sharply and nips the girl's leg and she cries out, arms flailing. Blood draws and tears follow. High-pitched screams echo throughout the pavilion. Tuffie senses every eye in the place bearing down on him. It's a heavy feeling. A fairly young, probably thirtyish, copper-haired woman in painted-on jeans runs frantically up to them just as Tuffie pulls the frightened child from the horse's back. He smiles at the woman. He bought her a drink once awhile back, but it went nowhere. She doesn't recognize him in his clown makeup. And maybe that's a good thing. They both bend down to examine the child's leg. He's afraid the lady might call the cops.

When the little girl looks down and sees the blood, she starts to scream again. The volume of it rattles Tuffie's insides and his hands shake uncontrollably.

"It's all right, sweet pea. You're gonna live. She nicked you is all. Nothin' to cry about or nothin'." He thought that in this particular circumstance the tag *sweet pea* sounded better, or at least more fatherly, than *kid* or *kiddo*.

"Sir, this is not a riding-pony," the woman says, pointing to the sign that reads *Please Do Not Touch the Animals.*

"She's a mean ol' bitch, ain't she?" Tuffie says to the little girl.

She smiles but not enough to stop the crying.

"Excuse me?" the woman says.

"The mare, ma'am. Not you. I haven't known you long enough to make that kind of judgment." He winks and shoots the woman a coy smile, forgetting that his painted face is still frowning.

She tilts her head and looks puzzled. He wonders if she recognizes him, and if he should say something.

A crowd begins to gather about. An EMT works his way through the people and begins dressing the girl's wound. After she's patched up, Tuffie bends down to give her a hug and tell her everything'll be okay. He feels weird doing this, almost fake, but he knows it's what's expected. Her screams have settled into choked back tears as she clings to his neck and buries her face into his curly, blue wig. Tuffie's knees ache. He has to stand, so he picks the girl back up into his arms and eases himself to his feet. He's woozy and his balance is off. She squeezes him tightly, and he does his best to not tip over.

"Nothin' to see here, folks," he says, addressing the crowd. "All my fault. I reckon I figured a filly named Peppermint would have herself a better disposition than that."

"It's not the horse's fault," the woman says.

Tuffie turns to her and stares just a little too long. The sun has aged her around the eyes since the last time he saw her, or maybe it was dark that night and he just didn't notice. Still, she's pretty.

"Never said it was, ma'am. I shoulda known better. Don't know what I was thinking. I take full responsibility. Blame it on the clown."

"Are you all right, sweetie?" the woman asks the child.

"I wanna…go home."

"What's your name, dear?"

"I wanna go home."

"She misses her momma," Tuffie says. The child is beginning to get heavy in his arms and beads of sweat gather on his brow. He sets the girl down and pats the top of her head like a dog. Wiping his forehead, he notices the chalk-white smear it leaves on his trembling hand. He wishes he could be anywhere but here. He wishes he hadn't polished off the flask, and, most of all, he wishes he knew what to do with this little girl. He looks at the woman, but her attention is still on the child. He's often wondered what his life would've been like if he had ever settled down and gotten off the circuit. Tuffie had known a few good women in his day, but the bad ones were always more fun. He wants to say something to this woman, but he doesn't know what. She looks good with the kid.

"Aw, poor thing," the woman says, stroking the girl's hair. She tries once more to connect with the child. "My name's Meredith. What's yours?"

"I wanna go home," she says again.

The little girl's words hit Tuffie square in the chest, bouncing around inside him. He feels for her and wishes he could give her what she wants.

"I know, kiddo. I know," he says. It's all he can think to say.

***

In the shade of the First Aid tent, they wait for the doc to return from lunch. The tears have stopped and so have the cries for home. The girl is back to ponies.

"Why did she bite me?"

"Because I scared her."

"Why'd you scare her?"

"Wasn't thinking, I guess."

She kicks her tiny legs back and forth in the chair like she's on a swing, and he gets up and begins to pace. He is full of nervous energy, peeking in the drawers and cabinets of the big red and white medical box the doc travels with. All the good stuff must be locked up. Tuffie wants a drink. He needs something.

"What are you looking for?" the girl asks.

"Nothing, just bored." He sits back down just as the doc enters the tent.

"Well, well, well, who is this pretty little thing? She's a bit young, even for you, Tuffie. What kind of trouble have you gotten yourself into this time?"

"Remember that waitress I used to run around with whenever we were in town?"

"The one with the teeth?"

"Yep, that's her."

"Hmm, yeah," says the doc, looking at the girl's face. He kneels down next to the girl and begins unwrapping the bandages. "Looks good to me—nasty bruise but nothing fatal," he says, rewrapping the leg.

"No stitches?"

"Nope."

"What about something for the pain?" Tuffie asks.

The doc shoots him a look like a son of a bitch.

"Tylenol's the best I can do for you, Tuff. You know that."

Tuffie shrugs. "Worth a shot."

"You still drinkin'?"

"Not drinkin' anymore," Tuffie says.

"You're just not drinking any less either, right?"

"You caught me."

The doc returns his attention to the girl. "Now, what's your name, little lady?"

She smiles but doesn't answer.

"Her name is Lilly. She's still taking all of this in."

"A pretty name for a pretty girl."

"My momma named me after The Who."

"She did? Well, how 'bout that? I always liked that song." The doc looks up at Tuffie. "What are you gonna do with her, Tuff?"

"Not sure yet. That gal that runs the ponies says she'll watch her during the show. After that, hell, I've got no clue."

"Meredith? She's a cute one all right," the doc says.

"Yeah, she sure is. I got her number, but I'm pretty sure she just gave it to me because of the kid."

"That sounds about right. I know that gal. She's not likely to put up with the likes of you," the doc says and then turns back to the girl. "I hope you're not afraid of the ponies now. Please tell me you're not, Lilly. I mean, ponies are a little girl's best friend."

"No. It was my daddy's fault. He scared her."

Again, the doc shoots Tuffie a look.

"What can I say? I'm a natural at this dad stuff."

"Yeah, I bet," the doc says. He stands up and starts to root out a sample pack of Tylenol from the cabinet and hands it to Tuffie. "Can you do me a favor, Miss Lilly?"

The girl smiles and nods.

"I know it's a fulltime job and all, but please try to keep your old man out of trouble if you can. He's known to make bad decisions."

"I'll try."

The doc pats the girl on the head and gives her a cherry lollipop from his shirt pocket. "That's all anybody can ask for," he says.

***

The girl is now suspicious of ponies but no less fascinated. She approaches with caution. Tuffie is proud as the little girl makes her way forward.

"Tough little cookie, ain't she?"

The woman nods. "We'll ease her in with some of our more docile ponies before trying to introduce her to Peppermint again. That was a really dumb thing you did."

Tuffie throws his hands up and does a goofy little dance for the woman. "Do I look like a smart man?" he asks, hands waving in the air.

"Point taken. Don't worry about her. She'll be fine."

"I sure appreciate your help, Meredith. This is all sort of sudden, and I got no idea what the heck I'm doing."

"Clearly," she says.

"Anyway, tell her I'll be back for her."

"Will do." She brushes her hair from her face and starts to say something but wavers.

"What?" Tuffie asks.

The woman looks at the girl and then back at Tuffie. "Be careful out there."

"Don't worry about me. I'm a tough ol' bird." He turns and starts to walk away.

"It's not all about you, Tuffie," she says.

He nods and keeps walking.

***

On his way to the main arena, Tuffie can't stop thinking about Lilly. What is he supposed to do with her? This is no place for a kid—always on the move, never planting roots. The rodeo-life is as hard on families as it is on bodies. How many more years did he realistically have left before he's too old to jump in the barrel? All it takes is one time. One miss. And then what? It's all over. That's what.

In the tunnel that leads out to the arena, Tuffie passes a bottle with an old-timer named Slim Mitchell he knew back in his own bull riding days. Slim is now a security guard and has put on a chunk of weight since the last time Tuffie saw him. Each sip of whiskey eases Tuffie's mind more than the one before. He's down to one pill, and the one he just took is already starting to work its magic. They talk about bulls and wild nights and even wilder women.

"So, what's it like?"

"Security? Sitting 'round mostly. Not much action."

"That doesn't sound half bad."

"Yeah, but I miss the circuit. The dirt and the shit and the way it all useta make my heart beat like it was gonna jump right out of my shirt. Rodeo is hard, but goddamn it's fun."

"That's what I'm afraid of, missin' it."

"I'll be perfectly honest, Tuff. Some days, I get so damn bored I start thinking about eating a shotgun slug for dinner."

"Jesus, Slim. That bad?"

"Sometimes." Slim takes a pull from the bottle and hands it back to Tuffie. "Of course, not being crippled has its perks, too."

"I hear that." This is a hard fact of the rodeo. Injury is unavoidable. Tuffie takes a pull himself and hands it back to his friend. "Hey, Slim, you got any kids?"

"A couple with my ex-wife, but they don't talk to me." Slim takes a drink and then stares down at the ground, kicking it with the tip of his boot. "I tried being a dad for a while—wasn't any good at it."

"Yeah, I'm not sure I'm cut out for it myself. What happens if I fail?"

"You fail. Your kid gets all sorts of screwed up, and blames you for every bad thing that ever happens to'm. But, hell, that could just as easily happen even if you're good at it."

Tuffie takes the bottle from Slim's outreached hand and lets these words rattle around. "Gawd, I hope I don't fail."

"You will, but just do the best you can and hope it all works out."

"Thanks, bud." Tuffie starts to take one last swig, hesitates, and decides not to. He hands the bottle back to Slim and says, "Well, I reckon I better get out there and earn my paycheck before they find some kid dumb enough to replace my old broke-down ass."

"I hear that."

***

With all its padding and the dirt that gathers inside during a competition, the aluminum barrel weighs close to one hundred and fifty pounds and Tuffie is already winded from rolling it around the ring. The interior padding is minimal compared to the spongy corporate sponsored outside. This is because bulls are much more valuable than barrelmen—another fact that is not lost on Tuffie. Also, the barrelman needs room to maneuver while inside, adjusting for various blows and attacks. The key is to brace yourself—to be ready for anything. The world will shake and all a barrelman can do is hang on and pray. That is, if he's into that sort of thing. Tuffie never has been.

The early events are pretty tame—barrel racing, roping, and pole bending. There's a bit of action with the saddle broncs when a rookie gets hung up and has to be freed, but by the time Tuffie arrives on the scene the rider is already loose. Tuffie plays the straight man for a couple of Goober Wilson's classic bits and spends the rest of the time waiting for the bulls. Wilson is a rodeo icon. An actual clown. A real funnyman. And the people love him. Children wait in line to have their picture taken with him for five bucks a pop like some kind of shopping mall Santa, and he gets to keep all of it. It's a racket. All of the glory and none of the hospital bills. Everybody loves a funnyman. Tuffie lost his first wife to a funnyman.

As he waits for the bulls, Tuffie wishes he had taken that last drink Slim offered. Then he wonders what Lilly is up to—probably playing with the ponies. She's not that bad of a kid—cute. He looks down and makes two fists. It's the only way he can stop his hands from trembling when they get like this. He releases them, and the shaking begins again. He could really use a drink.

***

The average bull weighs around two thousand pounds, one ton of pissed off hoof and horn, and it packs one hell of a wallop. Tuffie once heard a fellow barrelman compare the impact to that of a Toyota Corolla going about forty miles an hour, and thought it sounded about right. Inside the barrel, it's chaos—horns and legs and hooves shooting in. The slightest wrong move and an inexperienced barrelman can get caught. There's only one way out and the bull knows it.

The first three rides of the night go off without a hitch. The fourth is trouble. A twenty-three-hundred-pound Brahma named *Satan* is led into the chute.

"He breathes fire and devours bull riders for breakfast, folks," the announcer tells the blood thirsty crowd. These are the same people that watch NASCAR for the wrecks.

This particular bull has given Tuffie and the boys a few scares in the past, but the riders love him because he means big points. The kid that drew his card tonight is no slouch. He's got a few buckles and knows what he's doing. Tuffie looks up at the Jumbotron. Almost all the cowboys wear helmets and rib protectors these days. Better to be safe than fashionable. The camera zooms in on the rider's face, though partially hidden behind the mask. Of course, in Tuffie's day, a guy would have been laughed out of the arena for wearing all that protective shit, which is why all he sports are elbow and knee pads.

Inside the candy-red metal chute, the rider mounts the beast, easing down and securing his left hand with the rope. He inches forward and sets his feet, digging his heels into the bull's body. The bull is restless—snorting and rocking the chute. The cowboy gives the signal with his free hand and the gate swings open. The party begins—kicking and spinning and lurching back and forth. Tuffie readies himself as the bull unleashes every ounce of its bovine fury upon the rider clinging on for a chance at the money. Tuffie watches the scene like a hawk. Six seconds. Seven seconds. Eight seconds. Finally, the buzzer blasts the cheering crowd, and the announcer congratulates the rider on a great performance. Tuffie sees something's not right. When the rider tries to dismount, he doesn't quite clear the animal. The beast turns on the kid and the bullfighters run in to try and intervene. Tuffie grabs his portable fence and dances a goofy jig in front of it to distract the bull. The crowd cheers. The jig works, and the bull shifts its attention to Tuffie. He turns to scramble behind the fence but loses his footing and eats a mouthful of dirt. Somehow the charging bull misses him and launches the little picket fence into the air. It lands fifteen or twenty yards off and bounces several times. The crowd loves it. Tuffie's now breathing so hard he can't even think straight.

One of the bullfighters runs to the fallen rider and begins to help him up. The other tries to help Tuffie back to his feet. The bull is about to make a second pass and the two men sprint in opposite directions—the bullfighter one direction and Tuffie the other. The bull chooses Tuffie. He's slower than the bullfighter. His knees feel like they could buckle at any second. The barrel is close, but is it close enough? Tuffie goes for it, diving hands first, up and in. He doesn't have much time before the hit. He squirms to get in position and presses his body out against the barrel, flattening himself along its inner curve, and then pushing back with his head to reduce the force of the impact, but the bomb shelter can only do so much to protect against concussions. The hit is massive. The barrel goes airborne, spinning through space with Tuffie plastered inside.

Everything goes black.

***

When he comes to, Tuffie is lying on a long table in the backstage area. The little horse-faced girl is the first thing he sees. He can't think of her name, but he knows she's his.

"I guess your momma was right," he says. "That bull sure told me what for, didn't he?"

"Did you scare him?"

He laughs and feels a sharp pain on his right side—probably busted ribs. He clears his throat and spits blood on the floor. “I reckon I did, but not near as much as he scared me.”

“It’s good to be afraid,” she says and smiles at him. Her horse-like teeth are the most beautiful thing he has ever seen.

He smiles back. Every bone in his body is sore, even his jaw, but he feels proud and he can’t help himself. She learned something today—something he’d taught her.

“You’re damn right it is. And how were them ponies?” he asks.

“Amazing.” The girl becomes excited as she speaks. “I got to pet them all and Miss Meredith let me ride Pocket, Twilight, and Peppermint.”

“Peppermint? I’m surprised you went anywhere near that vile beast after what she did to you.” He sits up on the table and the room begins to spin like an out of balance ceiling fan on the lowest setting. The barrel has done a number on him.

Tuffie gives the girl a wink and a grin, and she smiles back. It’s warm and somehow makes him feel a little better about things.

“What’s say you and me blow this pop stand before that hack of a doc comes in here and tries to remove my liver,” he says and pats her on the shoulder. “Sound like a plan, kid?”

She nods.

“Hey, you hungry?” he asks. “I mean kids have to eat, right? You like corndogs? Funnel cakes? What do you eat?” He hops down from the table feeling broken but good. The girl meets him with a hug around the thighs. He feels her squeeze him with everything she's got. "Hey, you're strong for a munchkin, ain't ya?" he says. "Careful, you're liable to break an old man's legs huggin' like that." He limps forward a couple of steps. He is unsteady, but feels the girl trying to brace him. He looks down at her. There is something strangely comforting in that sweet little horse face. He doesn't know what it is, but he likes it. "Yeah, we'll grab ourselves something to eat and you can tell me all about the ponies, sweet pea."

"My name is Lilly," she says.

"I know, kid. Just like The Who song."

"Can Miss Meredith come with us?"

Tuffie laughs and grabs his side where it hurts.

"We'll see," he says.

MEAT

Their voices rang violent and the plates clashed together on the brink of fracturing. The sounds of your parents' marriage carried past the leftover pot-roast and spread throughout the house. In this particular memory, you sat so close to the television that you were absorbed into its wooden cabinet. A giant treasure chest of light and sound, it wasn't just a television set; it was the only piece of furniture that came to life, and it was there that you first learned of sex, and where girls became less icky.

At the time, everyone always talked about Farrah Fawcett-Majors, but you preferred Kate Jackson—the tall brunette. You got in trouble for kissing Katie Johnston on the playground at preschool. Her hair was shoulder length and brown, like Jackson's. A Betamax recording of the first *Police Academy* movie became your prized possession because of a few seconds of exposed boob that you were drawn to like a fat kid to cake until you traded up for a secondhand copy of *Body Heat*. You had entire issues of *Playboy* memorized cover to cover. Then came "Skinamax."

Your father's *sex talk* was brief if anything.

"We have cable," he said. "You probably know about as much as I do by now. Just be careful and don't fall in love."

To this day, you have never dated a blonde.

***

Still not used to the weight of the engagement ring, your thumb obsessively picks at it like a scab. You finish packing but feel like you've forgotten something. Like a disturbance in the Force, the wind rustles outside. A front is coming. Fuck it. You're already running late. The house is cold, even for January. The heater struggles to keep up. Jillian is in the kitchen fixing breakfast tacos, which is another way of saying that she's making black bean burritos that will be served before the noon hour. You can't remember the last time you had eggs. Or steak. Or bacon. Real bacon, not that soy shit.

In the kitchen standing over the sink, she is wearing nothing but an apron. This tells you she has intentions that go beyond breakfast. Guy Clark sings "Dublin Blues" on the radio. You approach her from behind, slide your hand softly around her taut belly, and kiss her gently on the neck. She leans into it and giggles. She is barely showing.

"Good morning to you, too," she says, and turns to face you.

"I know what you're doing," you say, and she smiles at this.

"I'm making you breakfast. Why so suspicious?"

"Because you did this the last time I had to go out of town."

She puts on her best pouty face and puppy dog eyes, bottom lip protruding and slightly upturned. "Did what? Got all sexy and fucked your brains out so you missed your stupid flight? Sorry for the inconvenience."

"Jesus, Jillian, don't get all huffy. Besides, this time I'm driving and Sid's already there to set things up. It doesn't matter when I leave."

"It's supposed to snow, you know?" She stops herself and looks up at you. "Really? It doesn't matter?"

"Well, within reason." You give her a wink and a well-rehearsed crooked smile that you stole from Harrison Ford.

Her eyes brighten and she presses her body into you and wiggles her hips. "That sounds subjective. I can work with subjective."

"I bet you can."

***

A week before the Spring Break of your freshman year of high school, a friend brought to your attention that Liz Taylor, the up and coming volleyball star, not the actress, thought you were cute. You didn't know who she was but quickly found out and, just as quickly, decided that you thought she was cute, too. At 5'11", she stood several inches taller than you—all legs. These were not a child's legs. These were a woman's. Her calves were strong and shapely. Her thighs led to the gates of Heaven. Your hands crawled ever upward as you kissed her awkwardly on the beach, always wondering what to do next—always fumbling forward. Her breasts were small but perfectly cupped, and she slobbered when she kissed. At the time, you honestly believed you loved her.

In the three years that followed, she held the carrot of her virginity just out of reach. Her virtue impenetrable. There were days when you got close but never quite there. She allowed you to satisfy her urges without the slightest hope of reimbursement. She did kiss it once, leaning over you across the Indian blanket covered bench seat of your grandfather's '72 F100, feeling frisky after a Dwight Yoakam concert. She had a thing for country music and cowboys, and you started wearing boots and pearl snaps. Your grandfather passed away and you lobbied for the truck. You got closer to Liz's treasure but couldn't seal the deal. Still, you waited.

On April 23rd, 1994, at Corey Ackerman's party, you finally got your shot. It is a memory you wish you could forget.

"I think I'm ready," she whispered to you in the backseat of Jason Wolf's parked blue Honda Civic out in front of the Ackerman's modest mini-mansion, her voice nearly swallowed by the twang of Hank Williams Jr. rattling through the speakers. She sat so close she was practically on top of you. Her hand brushed against your crotch as she squeezed your leg and you became erect. It was all you could think about for the rest of the night. Equally excited and terrified, you drank cheap whiskey and chased it with lukewarm Budweiser. At around eleven, she came and got you—retrieved you really. She grabbed you by the belt buckle and pulled you up the stairs and toward the spare bedroom, her thick calves flexing and releasing with each step upward. Your eyes were glued to them. Your head bobbed to the beat of their rhythm. She began to tell you what she was going to do to you.

You had never seen this side of her before—dirty and predatory. You liked it.

Once inside the bedroom, she shoved you onto the bed and began a striptease, playfully throwing articles of clothing at you as she disrobed her long slender frame. She pulled a condom from her jeans before tossing them in your direction. Your undressing was much less dramatic and choreographed than hers—far more frantic—like a matter of life and death. She approached, and you met her just in front of the foot of the bed. The kiss was brief but wet. Her kisses were always wet. She worked her way down your body, leaving a trail of saliva heading south. You trembled and your heart raced.

"You have to tell me if you're about to do it," she said, looking up at you.

"I will. I promise. I'll tell you right before."

She leaned in and pursed her lips slightly before slowly opening her mouth. You tried to think of baseball and state capitals, but instead you thought of Kate Jackson.

"Oh, shit." These were the only words you could get out before convulsing and losing all control.

"Oh, my God, I can't believe you did that, you asshole." She pawed blindly at her face. You stood there before her, frozen in shame and guilt—naked.

"I'm sorry. I'll get you towel," you said under your breath and stumbled toward the bathroom.

After considerable pleading, Liz agreed to give you another chance, but the whiskey had left you as anatomically useless as a Ken doll. She promised she'd never tell anyone. Instead, she told everyone. Now, two decades later, whenever you run into people from high school, this incident is the only thing they can remember about you.

You do not attend the reunions.

***

Jillian is resting her head on your shoulder. Your arm is falling asleep. She plays with your chest hair and tries out baby names. You are trying to list the presidents alphabetically in your head. When you get to Wilson you will make your exit.

"What about Sage? It works for a boy or a girl."

You say nothing, and so she continues to talk.

"How 'bout Madison?" she asks, and you think of James Madison.

This throws you because you're up to Rutherford B. Hayes and for some reason you always struggle with Hayes.

"What? God, no. Do you want her to grow up with daddy issues and become a porn star?"

"What about for a boy?"

"Madison? Are you kidding? Insert the exact same response but replace *her* with *him* and *porn star* with *giant pussy*."

She laughs a little and punches you in the shoulder. It hurts more and is less cute than you let on.

"Gross. You know I hate that word." This is the same girl who just spoke of *fucking your brains out* less than an hour earlier. Now she's sensitive.

"Sorry, babe. I forgot that your delicate little ears prefer the term *lady garden*. As in, may I please place my gentleman sausage in your lady garden?"

She laughs and punches you with a little less violence—more playful than painful.

"It's just that one word, silly. Well…that…and the c-word."

"Refresh my memory. Which word is that?"

"Stop it."

"Is it *cancer*? I hate that word, too." You pause for effect. "*Kaleidoscope*? Wait, no, that's a K."

"You know what word I mean. And don't you have somewhere to be?"

"I do, but that doesn't mean I don't have enough time to plant a little something in your lady garden before I go." You catch yourself saying these words just a second too late. You wonder what you're doing. You have five hundred miles and a snow advisory ahead of you. You've been waiting for your out—your chance to leave. She gives it to you, and now you pull this shit. What's wrong with you? Besides, haven't you already planted enough in her garden?

"It's not *that* little," she says.

One more round and then you hit the road. At some point on this trip, you are keenly aware your odometer will flip over back to one.

***

Alex Goodwin had been your campus tour guide when you visited the University of Texas that day in mid-June before your freshman year. Being a former cheerleader and long distance runner, she was a tiny, tan spitfire from Floydada, and she had a soft spot for boots and pearl snaps and boys who wore them, especially in the summer.

"That takes dedication," she told you.

You decided to take this as a compliment. At the end of the tour, you asked for her number and she gave it to you. After moving into your dorm in late August, you worked up the nerve to call her. She answered, and you kept her laughing for two straight hours—a college girl. The best part, she had only ever heard of one Liz Taylor.

A week later, you lay naked on her couch as she told lies to her boyfriend back home over the phone. Don Williams crooned softly on the small white RCA stereo that sat jammed into a bookcase on the other side of the room. You were no longer a virgin. You'd done it, not particularly well, but you'd done it. And what you lacked in skill you made up for in effort and willingness to learn. She kept you around for a few months and then gave you the talk. Her boyfriend was coming to visit, and your jealousy showed.

"You know you and I are *just* friends, right? I mean I've always been clear with you about that. Jacob is my boyfriend. I love him."

"And what are we?"

"I told you we're friends that fool around sometimes, that's all. It's cool, right? Are you still my friend?"

You agreed to remain friends because at the time you didn't know any better. That weekend you punched three holes in your closet door after thinking about *your friend* and her boyfriend wrestling beneath the sheets. Your knuckles bled. On Tuesday, you told her you were in a fight with two frat guys. She's never questioned you on this.

In truth, you've only ever been in two real fights and your record is split, one and one.

***

It hasn't started snowing yet, but it's coming. Finally, you get out the door and on the road. Immediately you feel guilty for lying to Jillian. After all, she'd kill you if she knew that the Ornamental Plant and Turf Conference in Amarillo was just a front to get out of town and that your old friend Alex from college, who you were meeting there, was actually a woman—a presumably still-gorgeous, confident, and freshly divorced woman.

Sex with Alex is not your intention. You're as loyal as a Labrador. And yet, somewhere in the back of your mind, you feel yourself clinging to the possibility. And with Alex, there's always a possibility.

The girl next to you at the corner of Oltorf and South 1st honks the horn of her dark green Subaru Outback to get your attention. It's an older model than Jillian's. The girl is cute but blonde—mid-twenties. She's wearing mittens. You lean across the cab to roll down the window. The cold air rushes in and your breath becomes visible.

"I love your truck," she yells.

"Thanks. It's a '72—all original, even the paint."

The original paint is both a thing of great pride and great concern for you. The truck's paint *is* all original, but you usually tell people that it's Tampico Yellow (Ford Color #2157). You say this knowing full well that it's not true. According to your VIN number and all of your grandfather's paperwork, your truck is actually Yuma Yellow (Ford Color #2214), a much brighter yellow than the duller #2157 shade that your truck now appears to be. Forty years of basking in the Texas sun has faded the factory paint job into a completely different color, shifted it into an all new identity. Plus, people make fun of the way you say the word *Yuma*. As long as this truck is around, you'll live in fear that someone will call your bluff on this color discrepancy, but no one ever has. The girl at the light is no different. She doesn't care about factory paint jobs. She smiles at you, rolls up her window, and waves as the light changes. She turns right onto South 1st and disappears up the road. You continue forward, bouncing the classic Ford around the tight narrow rolling curves of Oltorf until you get to Lamar and turn left towards Ben White so you can fight your way to the Y. This isn't the best way to go, but the Y is inevitable.

The Yahoo Maps directions Jillian printed for you while you were showering this morning say that it'll take you seven hours and thirty-four minutes to drive the 504.18 miles to the Texas AgriLife Research and Extension Center in Amarillo, but more than likely you'll just meet up with Alex and Sid at a bar somewhere nearby. Jillian doesn't like it when you drink, and so you don't. You doubt that Alex or Sid will allow this as an acceptable response, and so you have been mentally preparing to pace yourself, knowing that your tolerance isn't what it once was while Alex's has probably gotten higher.

In your mind, this trip is your bachelor party since Jillian put the kibosh on those hopes shortly after accepting your proposal. This is not your fiancée's first rodeo. She, like Alex and Sid, is divorced. Her first attempt at matrimony came to an abrupt end about nineteen months in when she found out her husband had remained in touch with one of the strippers from his bachelor party. You wondered what *remained in touch with* really meant, but refrained from asking, and accepted this as the reason why you were not allowed to have a bachelor party. Then, a few weeks later, you thought you'd give it another shot.

"What if we don't have strippers?" you asked.

"And then what would you do?"

A valid point. *Hey, guys, it's gonna be a great party. No booze, but all the veggies and soy-based meat substitutes you can stuff down your fat gullets.*

Since meeting Jillian, she has systematically removed every single vice that ever made you interesting. You could never subject yourself, much less your friends, to the absolute boredom and disappointment of a Jillian-approved bachelor party.

"We could get a clown," you said, and she smiled, but only because she knew she'd won. The mention of *clowns* is often much funnier than the appearance of an actual clown, and Jillian's inability to appreciate a good clown reference has always bothered you. This is when you began cooking up the conference alibi. Sid was on board.

You look down at your truck's gauge cluster. Your odometer reads 99,492.8 and counting.

***

One day, you decided to take your father's advice and stopped falling in love. Girls came and went after you finally gave up on Alex and said, "He can have you." This hurt her more than she'd ever admit—you know this now. You've picked it up from things she's said over the years. Of the many girls who drifted through your life during this period, the only one that ever stuck was Hailey Galloway. Actually, the word *stuck* isn't quite right. It doesn't do justice to the absolute adhesive power of Hailey's character. An addictive little pixie-flowerchild, she hid behind her big brown eyes and her long pasty twig-like legs. She was an atheist who genuinely feared God, or at least His existence—the idea that she might be wrong. You found her apparent unconditional love for you both endearing and repulsive at the same time. What she lacked in personality, she made up for in timing. Your paternal clock had begun ticking and your instincts were telling you to start settling down, find someone—a partner.

Perhaps it was your subconscious urge to nest that lured you away from your friends that April evening at the bluegrass festival, planting you right in front of Bela Fleck, though it's more likely that you were drawn there by the combination of two hits of LSD and the beautiful rainbow of reflections that shot out from Fleck's electric banjo. She, too, was alone, and she shared her water and pot. After the show, you bought her a veggie burrito from a vendor to say thank you. She didn't look like much—kind of cute in a way. Her style was that she had no style. Her clothes never fit her waifish figure quite right, always hanging unflatteringly one way or the other. Naked, however, she was perfection. If you could paint, you would have painted her. Her exposed image is etched in your brain under the header: *Things I Pray I Never Forget.*

Despite your best efforts to avoid making any kind of real commitment to Hailey, you moved in with her for practical reasons: her roommate had moved out and your lease had run its course. The grow room had been her idea. She held a degree in Horticulture from Southwest Texas and had been growing and dealing on a small scale for a number of years. With her experience and green thumb, Hailey became the brains of the operation, and you were the manual labor. She drew up sketches of shelves and dividers. You built them to spec.

Hailey fancied herself a purest, which meant no hydroponics or chemicals. She was a soil and guano kind of girl. This posed a problem as the summer approached. She'd already bought you both tickets for a string of west coast Phish shows, and she wasn't about to miss them. Besides, it'd be a great money-making opportunity. The plants were timed so you'd harvest two weeks before departure. This would leave enough time for the pot to dry and the next round of clones to root. The problem was that neither of you trusted any of your friends to plant-sit. You set to work on figuring out a way to regulate the new plants' water intake. As the plants grew, they'd need more water; this would be a crucial time in their grow cycle. After many failed attempts and trips to Home Depot, you invented a sensor that reads how dry the soil is and then releases a measured amount of water according to the dimensions of the flower pot in which it is contained. Hailey was impressed, and even you had to admit it was quite brilliant.

Over the next seven and a half years, you and Hailey churned out crop after crop of the best pot Austin, Texas has ever seen. It was the closest you'd ever been to being married until your current engagement. Playing house with Hailey had its ups and downs, but mostly it was good. She played the accordion but would only practice when you weren't at home. An amazing cook in spite of her vegetarian diet, and, unlike some people, she never once asked you to deny your carnivorous cravings; she just wasn't going to cook it for you. Hailey's objection to meat had nothing to do with animal rights, morality, or even health concerns. She just didn't like the way it felt in her mouth. She still ate bacon, but never ordered it. She picked it from your plate instead. Who ever heard of a vegetarian who eats bacon? You decided to ask her about it.

"Bacon keeps you humble," she said.

You laughed.

"Yeah, my grandmother actually had that embroidered on a throw pillow: *Bacon Keeps You Humble*. I wonder whatever happened to that pillow."

Life with Hailey was nice. It was simple. It was easy. She was perfectly sweet to you in every possible way, but she never challenged you and you got bored. The thing about Hailey was that you always knew you weren't really staying—just passing through. In the end, the breakup was amicable and profitable for both parties. She got the house, the pot, and all the connections. You took your drip system to market and finally became legitimate in your father's eyes; though, unbeknownst to him and your new fiancée, you still buy pot from Hailey. She charges you full price but acts like it's good to see you.

You saw Alex three times during your years with Hailey.

***

By the time you reach Llano, you're already hungry for lunch. There's a barbeque joint Sid told you about, but you can't remember the name.

Dude, I know you're all veg-e-table-arian now and shit (Sid always says it this way), *and I would be too if I had girl that looked like Jillian at home telling me what to do, but if you ever happen to grow your nuts back, you've got to drive up to Llano and stop in at BLANK BLANK'S and get you some ribs. They're amazing—fall off the bone and melt in your mouth good. Tell BLANK I sent ya.*

Shit, nothing. Not a clue. Your habit of tuning your friend and business partner out has left you at a disadvantage. You can only listen to someone rail on your life choices for so long before you have to start filtering it out, especially when the person doing the railing is a forty-five-year-old two-time loser who has been forced to move back in with his mother in order to keep up with his alimony payments. Sid is a cautionary tale. This is what having *nuts* gets you.

As you roll into town, you spot a place on the right that seems to fit Sid's description, *Laird's*—not a *BLANK BLANK* at all. The place looks like a house with picnic tables and a shaded area in the side yard that appears to have one of Sid's water misters going around it. You pull in and park. Before exiting the truck, something strange comes over you. It's excitement. It's guilt. It's the combination of the two. It's the same feeling you felt when you spoke to Alex on the phone about getting together this weekend.

Inside, the front room is crowded by a maze of tables and chairs. Red and white picnic checkerboards seem to be the running theme. An old man in an apron introduces himself as *Kenneth.* His handshake crushes yours with old man strength. He has no idea who Sid is, but he is still quite friendly in a rough abrasive kind of way. By this point, you know what you're about to do. You know why you're there. The smell of ribs and brisket surround you like a posse in an old western. This must be what it feels like to go to a whorehouse. You throw up your hands in defeat and order a jalapeño sausage sandwich to go and choose Cheetos as your chip option with an ice tea to drink.

In the car, the sandwich is messier than expected, but it is also the single sweetest thing that has ever touched your poor meat deprived lips. You lick your fingers clean as you navigate the steering wheel with your elbow and knee. Less than an hour later, you make a pit stop in Brady and spend thirty-seven minutes in the handicapped stall of the Walmart bathroom. You know exactly what caused this unscheduled stop but refuse to admit it, choosing to blame the morning's black beans and coffee instead.

Twenty-one miles from Eden, you stop again. Though the bathroom is worse, the overall experience proves less unpleasant. Still, you feel obligated to purchase something, and so you grab a 32 oz. lemon/lime Powerade and set it on the counter.

"I'll take this and a Mega Millions—cash option."

"You want the Megaplier with that?" the plump southern belle behind the counter asks.

"No, thanks. I'm not that lucky." This line gets a laugh almost every time you use it. Today it's just a courtesy smile, but you'll take it.

"You know we got the two for three dollars special on those Powerades." The gum she smacks is neon green and darts around her mouth like an electric eel. "I'm just sayin'," she says.

You grab the second Powerade, pay the girl with the neon gum, and head out to the truck. You let the factory 302 warm up. Then, you let the truck's heater do the same before you shift the long arm into drive. According to the bank across the street, the temperature has dropped eight degrees since you left Austin this morning. You switch out your Wilco tape with *Yankee Hotel Foxtrot* on one side and *A.M.* on the other for Townes Van Zandt's *Live at The Old Quarter*. To your relief, the cassette does not begin with the excruciatingly long Dale Soffar announcement about how everything you could possibly need is *upstairs*. This is the beauty of analog. Instead, the tape begins in the third verse of "White Freight Liner Blues."

It's bad news from Houston. Half my friends are dying.

By the time "To Live Is to Fly" comes to an end and "She Came and She Touched Me" starts up, Eden is in your rearview mirror. You wonder if Laird's is the place that Sid told you about. You take another swig of Powerade and screw the cap back on. Due to its bench seat, the all original Ford F100 has no center console or drink holders.

Another mile rolls over on your odometer.

***

For a fat man, Sid Barker is nimble. You found him in a Craigslist ad. He was looking to hire some help for the summer rush, and without Hailey's money tree, you needed a job. Misting systems and drip systems follow the same basic principles, and so you were a natural. After the summer, when work began to lag, you told Sid about your drip system for watering indoor plants and were surprised by his response. He immediately saw the potential and offered to make you his partner for a small investment. The investment was eventually waived.

"I mean, why do they have to be indoor plants? How 'bout plants in general? Think outside the box, man," he told you. "Maybe we could even get a couple of those office building contracts downtown. You know the ones where they pay you to take care of their plants, only we don't have to do shit because your little techno-gadget'll do all the work. It's perfect."

Without Sid, you would have never met Jillian. It was his idea to attend that yoga class. You were supposed to be his wingman.

"Are you sure you can handle intermediate?" you asked, trying to give him one last out. "This stuff's harder than it looks. There's no shame in starting out with beginner and then working your way up. When I used to do this shit with my ex, I think we barely made it to intermediate and we'd been doing it a while."

The truth was that you lost interest in doing yoga with Hailey when you realized it wasn't as closely related to the Kama Sutra as you'd originally been led to believe.

"Screw that. I'm here to meet women and the odds that they'll be better looking in the intermediate class have to be exponentially higher—no fat chicks need apply."

"Um, have you looked in a mirror recently? You're not a skinny man."

"Oh, just because I'm overweight, I'm only allowed to date whales. What kind of racist shit is that?"

"Okay, first off, not *racist*. Secondly, I doubt there will be any *whales* in the beginner class." Just then, a red Mazda Miata pulled into the parking lot with two rather large women squeezed inside. You and Sid watched as they exited the vehicle in stretched out yoga pants and waddled towards the studio.

"No whales, huh? What do you call those?"

"Frisky hippos?"

"I don't care how frisky they are. I want no part of that action."

"I'm warning you this shit's gonna kick your ass, Sid."

"I think I can handle an hour of stretching," he said.

"We'll see."

You had your own mat leftover from your Hailey days. He did not and had to borrow one. This is when you first saw Jillian—tall, lean, and fit.

When she bent over to grab the loaner-mat for Sid, you became lost. Sid said something you didn't hear, but she did, and you gave her a look that said, "I'm sorry for my friend. He's not meant for public consumption." She smiled and led you both into the studio.

The polished wood floors were almost as reflective as the mirrors that lined the walls. You and Sid took the last remaining spots in the back row. Jillian adjusted the thermostat and changed the satellite radio to what you found out later was her *Jason Mraz* station before taking her place in the front of the room. Despite her music selection, you couldn't take your eyes off her. She was a perfect Jaclyn Smith/Kate Jackson hybrid. You recorded, filed, and followed each position she demonstrated. Your Downward Dog felt good, heels driving through the mat, sweat pouring from you. Something about her voice made you take your practice seriously. There was grace in the way you flowed through your Sun Salutations. When she offered the Crow as a bonus advanced move, you and one other student were the only ones to attempt it with any degree of success. You were showing off. Sid huffed and puffed beside you. You held the Crow as long as you could. And as you fell, Jillian brought her Crow into a full handstand, and then slowly rotated into a Wagon Wheel. Sid's breathing increased. He tried to clear his throat. He sounded like a car that wouldn't quite start. He coughed three or four times and collapsed.

When the EMTs asked if you wanted to ride along with your friend, you told them that he was only a "work associate" and that you weren't that close. You hoped Sid hadn't heard this, but if he did, then you hoped he'd understand that your denial of him was driven by the most primal and basic of urges. Jillian had offered you a ride and there wasn't anything you could do for the fat man. Besides, it turned out to be a false alarm.

Colognes and perfumes are discouraged at The House of Om Yoga Studios, but Jillian's citrus body lotion made her skin taste sweet and salty.

***

The mother of your unborn child refers to your friend and business partner as *Sid Shifty*. She thinks he's either trying to steal your ideas or ride your coattails. Sometimes you think she's right; however, without Sid's help and shameless hustling, the Smart Soil 750 sensor (SS750) would not be where it is today. Sid believes in your product, which is why he flew into Amarillo a day early to set up the Smart Soil booth. He's probably schmoozing some potential clients right now. You pass through Winters and Sweetwater. Justiceburg flies by, then Lubbock and Abernathy and Hale Center. Amarillo approaches. You check your odometer, afraid you've missed it—99,979.3—now .4.

I-27 is icy and slick. Occasionally you feel the Ford lose traction, the backend fishtailing across the neighboring lanes. As your odometer creeps closer to being reborn, you lean forward and grip the wheel tighter. Your knuckles lose their pigment and become ghostly white. The phone rings. It's Alex.

"Hey, what's up, kid? I'm almost there." You then explain the Sid situation to the best of your abilities, and Alex is understanding.

"You know I've got a couple of friends I could set him up with, if you think it'll help."

"They're not fatties, are they?"

She laughs. "Oh, he's one of those."

"Yeah, in fact, I wouldn't advise setting him up with anyone you intend on remaining friends with—just sayin'."

"Got it," she says. "I think I've got the perfect girl. Let me see what she's up to tonight."

Alex gives you directions to a Mexican restaurant near the conference that sells dollar margaritas.

"You're the best," you say before hanging up.

At exit #117, you ease off the interstate and onto Canyon Drive. At the light, you turn left onto Bell Street and proceed cautiously toward town. The snow is packed along the curbs and sidewalks. The phone rings again. It's Sid.

"Dude, are you here yet?"

"Almost. I was slow getting out of town."

"I bet you were. So, what's on the agenda for tonight?"

"Well, I told you I'm meeting that friend of mine from college."

"Right, the cheerleader," he says in a voice that's creepy even by Sid's standards.

You wish you'd never told him about Alex, but he would have figured it out eventually. It's easier this way.

"Well, you know me," he tells you. "I don't wanna cock-block you or anything, but we *are* having drinks tonight."

"I told you, it's not like that," you say.

"Sure it's not. I understand. You're tellin' Noah about rising water."

"It really isn't. How's the conference?"

"Good. I've got something big in the works."

"Really? How big?"

"Big enough it might keep you from having to work on Jillian's vegetable farm." His voice sounds optimistic.

"It's not a farm. It's a theme-based bed and breakfast."

"Eating produce is not a theme. It's a fucking salad."

"Look, I'm almost there. I'll talk to you in a minute." You give him the directions to the restaurant, and he tells you that you'll recognize him from having met him previously, and you laugh.

"Right. Sure, I will."

Inside the Aztec inspired restaurant, you find Sid sitting with Alex and another woman. How did he know? Sid is leaned in close to Alex and his back is turned to the other woman. Alex spots you and jumps up to meet you as you approach the group, throwing her arms around your neck and kissing your cheek several times.

"Hey, girl, damn it's good to see you," you tell her. She is visibly tipsy and overly affectionate. You sit down at the table, and Sid immediately turns his attention to the other woman who he's been ignoring up to this point. Her name is Denise. She's older but attractive. There is something desperate in her face, and you know Sid sees it, too. He calls the waiter over and orders another round of margaritas.

"So, what's this that Sid's been telling me about you getting your nuts chopped off? A vegan B & B, really? How rich is this girl?"

"You know those pink Cadillacs that peddle makeup to bored housewives?" Sid says. "Yeah, well, his fiancée is her granddaughter."

"Shit, you're kidding?"

"Nope. After our boy ties the knot and that baby pops out, she gets full access to her trust—boo-koo bucks, darlin'. He's set for life. Only, it's *her* life."

"Wow, I never pictured you as a kept-man." Alex's smile as she says this is coy, like it's more than just a smile.

"It's not as bad as it sounds. The place we're buying in Fredericksburg is gorgeous. I'm actually looking forward to it."

This is a lie, and you're pretty sure that your friends know it.

"And why vegan?" Alex asks.

"Because Jillian is the type that thinks just because she's a vegan, everybody else should be too," Sid chimes in. "Plus, you haven't heard the best part."

"Really? Do tell."

"In addition to running the vegan B & B, she also plans on devoting more time to her pottery. The idea being that they can sell these *works of art* to the guests as souvenirs. Even gonna teach classes. I mean, how could this *not* work?"

"You're not helping."

"Vegan? That's pretty specific. Don't you think that's kind of a narrow market?" Denise wants to know.

"An astute observation, my dear," Sid answers. "That's precisely what I keep saying. A better investment would be to put some of that money into our company—marketing and production—you've got to spend money to make money."

"Despite what my colleague is trying to lead you to believe, Jillian has also promised to invest—just not as much as Sid would like."

"Ten thousand's a fucking band aid. It's not a solution."

"I thought you had something big in the works?"

"I do, but nothing's final. We've got a meeting at one tomorrow."

Over the next hour, several pitchers of margaritas are ordered and drained. The idea that this weekend is your last moment of pure freedom begins to permeate and infect the spirit of the night. Sid wants to go to a strip club, but Alex has other ideas.

"So, when was the last time you ate meat?"

"This afternoon and it was amazing."

Alex smiles at you like she's up to something and asks, "When was the last time you had a steak?"

"God, I honestly can't remember."

"Steak it is."

The sign for The Big Texan Steak Ranch that you passed on your way into town advertises a 72 oz. steak challenge. The giant cow statue out in front of the actual restaurant also advertises this. You're pleased to discover that the Big Texan also has its own brewery. You tell Alex to order you a Pecan Porter and excuse yourself for the restroom. When you come back, you find them sitting in a booth—Sid squeezed in next to Denise—Alex waiting for you. The tablecloth is a dairy cow naugahyde number.

"We ordered for you," she tells you, and you know what this means.

Your attempt at the monstrous steak is valiant but ill-advised. The challenge is not just a steak. It also includes a baked potato, ranch beans, shrimp cocktail, house salad, and a buttered roll. Sid and the girls cheer you on, as well as the wait staff and several of the other customers in the restaurant. After finishing the salad and putting a sizable dent into the slab of beef, the meat sweats kick in and it becomes difficult to swallow. Failure to complete the challenge in under an hour will cost you $72. Alex dabs your forehead with her napkin like you're a prize fighter waiting for the next bell. You know you have gone as far as you can go, or at least as far you should go. You try to throw in the towel, but Sid won't let you. Instead, he informs you that the official current speed record on The Texas King challenge is held by Joey Chestnut at 8 minutes and 52 seconds. The unofficial record is held by a 500 lb. Siberian Tiger who devoured the meal in a mere minute and a half. You have been eating steadily for half an hour. You eat three more bites and immediately regret this decision. In fact, you regret almost every decision you've made up to this point. You have no choice. You are done. You are finished. No mas.

You begin to feel as though you are trapped on the teacup ride at Disney World, the room tilting and spinning uncontrollably. Alex sees that you're in bad shape and offers to take care of you. Sid also sees this but doesn't care. He has finagled a ride with Denise back to his hotel and has plans of his own. You stand to leave but are unsteady. Alex helps you to the door. There is a cinder-block motel with an old west theme connected to the restaurant and she gets you a room, escorting you inside with Sid's help.

"Remember we've got a one o'clock meeting, lover boy. I need you there," Sid says and shuts the door behind him.

When you wake, you find yourself stripped down to your boxer shorts. The spinning has stopped, but you still don't feel right. Alex lays naked, except for her lacy lavender panties, next to you on the king-sized bed. You notice that she has taken really good care of herself over the years and looks as good today as the day you met her, maybe even better. All you can remember from the night before is clinging to the toilet and praying for salvation. You may have even vowed never to touch meat again for as long as you live. There is a knock at the door. Alex stirs. It's housekeeping. You look at the red glowing clock and remember your meeting.

"Fuck, we gotta go."

You take a lightning fast shower and get dressed as quickly as you can. Alex is slow moving, but you herd her out the door and into the truck. It's snowing. The parking lot is a blanket of white. You don't wait to let your engine warm up. You shift into gear and the rear tires begin to spin, so you let up a little until they find some grip. The odometer is at 99,996.6.

As you zip along Amarillo Boulevard heading west, Alex is half asleep with her head resting on the passenger window. You can see the warmth of her breath on the glass. A stray dog darts out into the road and you swerve to miss it. The contents of the cab shift and flail. Alex is awake.

"Slow the fuck down," she says. "It's icy. We'll get there when we get there."

You realize that this meeting isn't just a meeting. It may be your last chance at an identity solely your own.

"Do you think it's okay to change yourself for someone?" you ask.

"I think we're always changing, whether it's for someone else or not. The key is not to lose yourself completely."

"Do you think that's what I'm doing?"

"I can't say. What do you think? Is running a vegan B & B your life's dream?"

"No, but it is hers."

Alex nods.

"Do you remember what you wanted to be when you were a kid?" she asks.

"Yeah, Bosely. You know, the guy from *Charlie's Angels*."

"How very heterosexual '80s male of you," she says.

"I know, right? It was either that or a rodeo clown." Alex laughs, and you look at her—your eyes locking momentarily.

The light ahead of you changes from green to yellow, and you go to press the brake, and it doesn't budge. Your heartbeat increases by several beats. You try again before turning your attention to the floorboards to investigate the issue. Your unopened bargain Powerade has lodged itself beneath your brake pedal. The light changes to red. The intersection approaches faster and faster, though you know your speed is constant. Your right arm instinctively extends to secure your passenger, as if you have the strength to offset the laws of physics. Alex braces herself for the impact. You kick wildly at the plastic bottle, finally knocking it loose. You apply the brake, but the icy conditions make this pointless. The crossing traffic is upon you.

You think of family dinners and pot roast and bickering, Reagan getting shot, and *Charlie's Angels* and *Police Academy* and *Body Heat*. You think of Liz Taylor's calves and Alex's white RCA stereo and Bela Fleck's banjo. You think about Townes Van Zandt and the word *virtue* and how you like the way it sounds but have always struggled with its function. You think about the way grass smells the first time you mow it every spring. The first time you ever tasted a Snickers ice cream bar. The taste of bacon. Hailey naked. Sid in the ambulance. And the first time you made love to Jillian. The way she smelled like something tropical. You think about the time the two of you made prickly pear jelly together and decided that the next time you'd choose a less violent fruit. The day she told you she was pregnant runs through your mind. You think of Kate Jackson. And that's it. That's life. It's a process. Without change, you are meat and nothing more.

The odometer on your Ford has already flipped. You missed it.

COFFEE WITH AVA

Nat Coughlin sat outside the coffee shop on 3rd smoking a menthol and scratching a string of lotto tickets over a folded copy of the *New York Times*. The morning's mugginess had given in to the heavy, oppressive heat of the day, and Nat had already thrown in the towel on the crossword, figuring he'd try his luck elsewhere. The cigarette hung low from the left corner of his mouth. Smoke seeped from his nostrils over a jungle of matted whiskers as he squinted and leaned forward to see if he'd won. He then leaned back in his chair, straightened, cleared his throat, and spat, just missing the store-bought combat boots of a kid holding the door for his girl and trying to sip coffee that Nat knew from experience was still way too hot.

"You'd better let that cool, son."

"You ain't kidding," the kid said, spitting onto the sidewalk.

"Yeah," Nat said, directing his speech to the young lady. "That's the sorta lesson a man's gotta learn for himself the first hundred times or so before it really kicks in, not unlike these damn donations I keep making to the 'Carolina Educational Fund,'" he said, tapping the lotto ticket on the table. He smiled. "You don't have to tell me. I know it'd be easier to just write'm a check, but what fun would that be?"

"No winners?" the girl asked.

"Not a goddamn thing—not even a buck for my trouble," the old man replied. His voice sounded like something from an old western, seasoned with grit and sandpaper, and the lines that spread across his face resembled a busted-up windshield on an old farm truck. "Can't say I'm surprised, though. I've never really been the lucky type. Ain't in my nature." He paused to sip his coffee before continuing. "Nah," he said peeking over the lip of his cup. "I'm the type that's number only comes up in the wrong kind of lottery. You know, the kind when they send you off to some godforsaken country to tramp through the rain praying for mercy and a dry pair of socks. That's my version of luck. Always has been."

The kid and his girlfriend both laughed.

"I know the feeling," the girl said.

"Yeah, well, I reckon most people do in one way or another." He gave the couple a quick nod and a crooked smile.

The boy was twenty-something, a kind of *new Bohemian* type that was typical for the kids of today. He wore a tight, plaid pearl snap shirt with the sleeves rolled up to expose his tattoos, which Nat estimated had probably cost the kid at least a grand, all told. His beard was long but well-manicured, and he had those crazy rings in his ears that stretched out the lobes to the point where a man could easily slide the handle of a Phillips-head screwdriver right through without touching a thing. The girl he was with was attractive, though only a few shades shy of anemic. She shared the boy's appreciation for body art, and her short black hair stood spiked and accented with a color of red not found in nature. Nat dusted the fruitless lottery shavings from his lap and gestured for the couple to take a seat, and so they did.

"Y'all ain't from around here, so I gotta ask. What brings ya to Smithfield?"

"Ava Gardner," the boy said, as the girl lifted a small bag into view that bore the words *Ava Gardner Museum – Smithfield, NC – USA*.

"Funny, wouldn've pegged y'all for fans. I mean, don't get me wrong. It's just y'all don't really fit the typical profile is all."

"My mother was obsessed with those old movies, so I'm kind of a fan by proxy. Plus, she named me after her, so I never really had much choice," the girl explained. She then glanced up at the boy, squeezed his hand, and said, "And I guess poor Brad here just got taken along for the ride."

"Sweetie, we all have a choice," Nat said. "It's just that sometimes we don't give it much thought. Take this boy you're with. Brad, is it? Did he come willingly on this pilgrimage, or did you have to threaten him?"

"Mostly willingly," she said and smiled. "There may have also been a small amount of implied bribery involved."

Nat nodded—taking it all in. "Threaten, bribed, or even just smitten, the boy made a choice to join you whether either of you knows it or not. That's the thing. When your number's called, every man has to make a choice."

She looked at Brad. He shrugged.

"So, not to pry too much into y'all's business, or nothing, but whatcha got in the bag, honey? A set of Miss Ava's earrings?"

"Nothing fancy like that. Just a mug." She pulled it from the gift shop bag and began to unwrap the coffee mug on the table, stuffing the white butcher paper back into the bag. When she had finally freed it, she handed the mug across the table to Nat for inspection.

The mug itself was white with a picture of Gardner in a lacy number, decked out in diamonds and red lipstick, against a pink curtain background. Her signature began atop her left breast and ran clear across her shoulder into the Pepto-abyss of the curtain. On the backside of the mug, the museum had printed its info just in case anyone had any doubts about where the mug had been obtained, and the tag that hung from the handle boasted a six-dollar asking price and claimed coffee to be an "essential part" of the starlet's success, her not being a "morning person" and all.

"Says here, you'll be lucky if your coffee tastes half as good as she looks. Of course, one can only presume they mean her as she was and not the decaying corpse she'd be today," Nat said, and chuckled to himself as he handed back the mug.

"Let's hope," the girl said, as she popped the plastic lid off her cup and began to pour the contents into the mug.

"You never know 'round here. After all, this is ghost country and stranger things have happened."

"Yeah, so we've heard," the kid said.

"Boy, you got no idea. Heck, I've seen some things that'd make the hair on the back of your neck stand up and testify to the Big Man himself."

"You talkin' Nam?"

"Might be. After a while, it all starts to blend together, and it gets tough trying to tell which part happened where. You know what I mean?"

"Not exactly," the girl said.

"Yeah, bud, you kinda lost me, too, on that one."

Nat leaned forward and arched his back as if to crack it back into shape, and then sat back in his chair and collected himself.

"Let's take Ava Gardner for example," he said, pointing to the mug in the girl's hand. "Back when I was still a little fella, my daddy took me and my older brother to the Johnston County Fair. At least, I think it was the fair. It might've been a rodeo or a circus or the like." He tilted his head and squinted up toward the sky as if he was trying to tell the time by the sun's location, and then shook it off. "They definitely had animals. I know that for a fact. Reason is, all my brother and me cared about was seeing Miss Ava Gardner, but we never got the chance."

"She was supposed to be there?"

Nat nodded. "Yep, her homecoming was the big attraction of the whole shindig, and they'd been playin' *The Killers* for a week straight over there at the Howell in preparation." He pointed up the road at the old single-screen theater. "You ever seen that one?"

"Hemingway, right?" the boy asked.

"Sorta. Let's just say Hollywood took some liberties, but then I guess they always do."

"It's the nature of the medium," the girl said.

"You got that right. Of course, I digress." He cleared his throat and hacked into his fist. "The point is that my daddy'd promised my brother and me he was gonna take us to meet Miss Gardner that day. And if you ever saw that movie, then you know that ol' Kitty Collins was the type of gal that'd turn a boy into a man real quick. A *femme fatale*, I think they call'm."

"So, what happened?"

"Funny story. See, my daddy was a farmer and a bit too preoccupied by his trade." Nat reached for his pack on the table and withdrew a menthol. "Y'all want one?"

"Nah, we got our own."

"Let me guess. Spirits?"

The kid nodded and reached for his own pack. Nat offered a light.

"So, anyway, we weren't at this fair thing for five minutes before we ran into our neighbors, the McCullers. And all they could talk about was this goddamn chicken. Said it was the size of a dog. And that's how everybody described it. Not bigger than a bread box or taller than a two-year-old—just the size of a dog. That's it. And my daddy just had to see it for himself." Nat scratched behind his ear for a second like a mutt going after a flea, and then rolled his neck back a forth a few times. "I mean, what's that even mean? Are we talking Rottweiler/Great

Dane big? Or, are we talking Pekingese? 'Cause that's quite a discrepancy there."

"Valid point," the boy said, probably wondering where this story was going. He looked to the girl for a way out.

"So, how big was it?" she asked.

"Dunno. Never saw the damn thing. We stood in that line all damn day waiting to see that chicken, and when it was our turn, I was too short see past the guy in front of me, but my brother saw it."

"And what'd he say?"

"Said it was about the size of a dog." Nat laughed and crushed out his cigarette in the ashtray.

"And what about Ava Gardner?" the girl asked.

"Never saw her. She was keeping cool, signing autographs, and handing out kisses under a tent, but we never made it over there in time."

"Bummer."

"Just the beginning of a life chalked full of disappoints and missed opportunities."

"Aw," the girl said.

"Well, not everybody gets to meet Ava Gardner. In fact, the vast majority of us don't."

"The world needs ditch diggers, too, right?" the boy added.

"Exactly. And I may not of ever met a Hollywood actress, but I've seen at least fifty ghosts in one sittin', and I *know* that's more than most."

The young couple exchanged glances but didn't say a word.

"I ain't pulling your leg. I swear, I seen it. At least once, maybe more. That's where things get fuzzy."

"How so?" the girl asked.

Nat rolled his lighter across his knuckles and let his eyes wander to an old Pontiac station wagon trying to parallel park across the street.

"Yeah, you can't start something like that without finishing it," the boy said.

Nat smiled and lit another cigarette. He leaned back and bellowed the smoke, glad they'd taken the bait.

"So, not long after the chicken debacle, my daddy tried to make it up to us. Told me and my brother he was taking us fishing out in the swamps east of town. Loaded us up in this dinky little boat one morning before dawn and off we went. It was spooky out there, like something weren't right. The trees were so dense they completely blocked out the moon and the stars, but it wasn't just dark. It was something else. You could feel it. You didn't know what it was, but you could definitely feel it. And as we're getting deeper into it, my daddy starts to tellin' us this story he'd heard when he was a kid."

The girl sipped her coffee from her Ava Gardner mug and brushed her foot across the boy's calf.

"And?" she asked.

"He tells us there's this island he's taking us to, and that it's got a history. Says back in the Civil War, sometime after Sherman had had his way with the area, there were all these bandits, like land-pirates, rapin' and pillagin'. And there was one group of'm that hit up this old colonel's place, a big old plantation. They were demanding money and gold and whatnot. And when the old coot refused'm, they strung up his wife. Then, they hung him from the same tree."

The couple leaned in, fully hooked by this point, and Nat hit his cigarette a couple of times in quick succession and exhaled in the same manner and waited for the smoke to clear before continuing.

"And as one can imagine, the colonel's son wasn't too pleased when he heard the news."

"I bet."

"So, this kid goes to his commanding officer and says he wants to put together a unit of about twenty men or so and hunt these fools down. And long story short, they found those bastards, all fifty of'm, hiding out on this little island in the swamp. The same one my daddy's takin' us to. And this kid was smart, 'cause he knew he's outnumbered, so he tells his boys to go find the rattiest clothes they can find for the raid."

"Why'd it matter what they were wearing?" the boy asked.

The girl reached into the boy's front pocket and grabbed herself a cigarette and lit it.

"'Cause," she said. "It's easier to sneak up on your prey when you look like he does." She smiled and winked at Nat.

"Spoken like a girl that's dawned the sheep's clothing a time or two," Nat said, and returned the wink.

She blushed.

"So, they get in their skiffs all dressed up like bums and head over to the island claiming to be Yankee bandits. And those dumb bastards welcomed'm right into their camp."

"Nice," the kid said.

"Damn skippy. That boy hung every damn one of'm, 'cept one."

"Really?"

"He saved the leader for last. Made him watch his boys choke out and shit themselves before giving him the pleasure of joining'm."

"Dang."

"Yeah, and maybe it was the moss or the swamp or just dumb youth playing a trick on my brother and me, but when we got to that island that morning, we saw something—fifty figures swinging from the trees."

"And you think they were ghosts?" the girl asked, setting her mug down on the table.

"Coulda been," Nat said. He then paused and stared at the picture of Ava Gardner. "Or, maybe I just *choose* to believe they were. Maybe that's just easier. You know, like the dead never leave us. Like all the soldiers and starlets, victims and bandits alike, are all still here floating around in the stories we tell children." He looked at the mug and then the girl.

She smiled.

"Don't you agree, Miss Ava?"

MAKING THE CALL

Big John Dalton, the former USC star running back, sits next to ex-Alabama great, Gino Swanson, at a long half-moon shaped desk with the letters *E-S-P-N* floating across a large television screen directly behind them. Both men are dressed in enormous, shiny suits, expertly tailored to stretch across their massive frames.

"And we're back with *College Football Breakdown*. Your source for all the latest drama in the soap opera we call college football. Set hut!" Gino fakes like he is dropping back in his swivel chair to pass. He turns and pretends to hit his cohost square in the numbers.

"Yes, welcome back, folks! And for those of you just joining us, here's what you missed before the break: My good friend, Gino, was *completely* missing the point on this whole Bergheim/TU thing. Now I'm not saying that Andy Bergheim hasn't done some amazing work at Southwest, 'cause he has. Nobody is denying him that. The Badgers are a completely different team than what they were a few years ago. I'm just not sure he's ready to coach, much less recruit, at the upper level yet, and TU is about as big as it gets."

"Are you saying you don't think Bergheim can handle it, Johnny?"

"Can Andy Bergheim handle it? I don't know. I just don't know." Big John throws his hands up as if he's asking for a sign from God: *Can Andy Bergheim handle it?*

"That's ridiculous, Johnny. Of course he can recruit at that level. And coach at that level? Really? Do you have to even ask that? He was Fischer's offensive coordinator for eight years. He's got two rings." Gino flashes his own National Championship ring to the camera. "You might have a Heisman, Big John, but only those of us who have brought home the title know what it takes to accomplish something like that." Gino fires finger pistols at his cohost, who pretends to be shot but quickly recovers and straightens back up in his chair.

"Yeah, but he wasn't the head coach of those teams. Fischer was."

"Maybe, but Bergheim called the plays. Look at what he's done so far. Southwest couldn't even buy a win before Andy Bergheim got there."

"They won a game."

"Who'd they beat?"

"They beat Rice that one year."

Laughter erupts throughout the studio.

"Oh, I'm sorry. I forgot all about them beating the other worst team on the planet. And what was the score of that game, Johnny?" Gino grins like he's selling toothpaste.

"I believe it was three to two."

"How 'bout that? A real barnburner, folks. If only the Owls could have gotten two safeties instead of just one, they might have had a chance." Gino wipes his brow with his signature Alabama crimson red handkerchief. "First off, let me say this to all the people out there in TVland: *Roll Tide*." He shakes his hand in the air like a preacher with a Bible.

"Really? You Bama boys are all alike."

"I'm just sayin'."

Big John shakes his head as Gino faces him.

"Let me ask you a question, Mr. Dalton. How *bad*, and by that, I mean *God awful*, does your offensive line have to be for the Rice Owls to score a safety on you?"

"Pretty dang bad, Gino."

"Ladies and gentlemen, I rest my case. Andy Bergheim brought them from nothing and he can save TU's legacy, too. He's *that* good."

"I get what you're saying, Gino. They were lousy before Coach got there and now they're the conference champs, but it's a weak conference. And I never said he wasn't a hell of a coach. I'm just not sure he's ready for TU, that's all. It's one of the biggest programs in the nation." Big John Dalton pauses for effect and takes a sip from his mug. "Heck, we don't even know if TU really wants him. We're just a couple of girls spreading rumors and talking out of class, Gino."

"They'd be crazy not to want him, Johnny. And I have every reason to believe this job offer rumor is legit. Bergheim is the real deal. It's more than just conference championships and undefeated seasons. He's preaching a new way of thinking and working miracles with it. This guy's an innovator. A genius. A straight up offensive mastermind and a leader of men. Those players at Southwest are buying what he's selling. Andy Bergheim is like Moses leading his team, whatever that team might be, to the Promised Land. Do I think the players at

TU are going to buy into what Andy Bergheim is preaching? Do I think the fans are going to buy into it?" Gino returns Big John's dramatic pause and raises him a tip of the mug before he takes his sip. "Yes, Johnny Dalton. Yes, I do."

Big John throws his hands up as if to surrender.

"All right. All right. How can I argue with a biblical reference like that? Just keep in mind they've still got a bowl game to play, Gino, and against a pretty tough Tiger squad that's been there before and has proven they can get it done when it counts."

"And the big question everyone is asking is: Will Andy Bergheim still be on the Badger sideline come January third when the mighty Badgers of Southwest suit up to take on the Tigers of Mizzou at the Pace Picante Bowl in New York City?"

"To TU or not to TU? *That* is the question," Big John says as he faces and points to the camera. "And your guess is as good as mine, America."

"Nice Shakespeare reference, big guy. But I was just thinking. Technically, I don't think Moses ever actually made it to the Promised Land." Gino tilts his head and playfully raises one eyebrow to the camera. "Did he, Johnny?"

"No, Gino, he didn't. Instead, he took the job at TU for buckets of cash and was never heard from again and that's probably what Andy Bergheim is going to do, too."

"Can you blame him if he takes the money?"

"Not one bit, Gino. Not one bit. The big dog has got to eat," and with that Big John nods to his cohost and smiles directly into the camera. "We gotta take a quick break, folks, but when we get back, Gino and I are going to breakdown the keys to the game."

"Badgers—Tigers. Stay tuned."

***

Andy Bergheim stood in front of the open freezer door spooning ice cream straight from the pint. Denali Moose Tracks, his favorite. The frozen air poured from the mouth of the appliance as he traced circles around the edge of the carton with his spoon. He tried to maintain a flat and consistent level of the contents with each bite, as if he were trying to hide his own tracks.

The ESPN analysts jabbering in the background theorized about his future, but the coach's mind was elsewhere. There's more to football than just football. He took the bottle of Jameson from the freezer door and set it down on the counter. The warmth of his hand left an impression on the frosted bottle. Uncapping it, he took a quick swig—cold and thick followed by a slight burn. Chasing it with a spoonful of moose tracks, an idea hit him: Whiskey/Ice Cream. Could be the best thing since Darrell Royal invented the Wishbone Offense. Bergheim then raised the bottle and topped off the carton with whiskey. He was now fully committed to the entire pint and mixing it into a thick shake-like substance. He took a bite. Amazing. Taking another, he headed back into the den to catch the rest of the show.

Strange to hear his name tossed around in such discussions. TU's offer was big money, more than he'd seen in all of his years of coaching combined; but, more importantly, it was a chance to compete on the national level—to really make a run at the Championship. It was a big program with big time recruiting potential—a once in a lifetime opportunity—everything he'd worked for—everything he'd dreamed of. And the timing was almost perfect. The move wouldn't be a problem. The kids were all out of the house, and Nancy had already given her full support—no surprise there. She'd always been so supportive through the years. And why shouldn't she? He was on the verge of making it. She'd never have to teach another art class again, not with the money TU was bringing to the table. Still, it was going to be rough going the first couple of years—building from the ground up. And then there was his current team to think about.

In only three years, Coach Bergheim had turned the program around at Southwest, 11-0 for the season and a trip to their first bowl game in school history. It was a big deal, and he felt like his boys were going to need his guidance to help them through all the hype that surrounds a game like that. Football is three-quarters mental, and as big as those boys are, they're still just kids. But TU wanted an answer by Friday. Two days. They might as well have said two minutes.

He understood the public relations side of it from the selection committee's point of view. A 3-9 record, with zero conference wins, creates a hostile environment—unacceptable for a school with TU's reputation. Their fans and alumni were calling for blood. They'd practically run Parsons out on a rail. The clock ticked, but why couldn't they at least let Bergheim finish what he'd started at Southwest? Was it really that urgent? Sure, he needed to start recruiting, but it didn't feel right to leave his boys in the lurch like this with only a few weeks till the Picante Bowl. He was the captain of the ship, and it was up to him to ensure that they stayed the course. And then, deep down, past all the sweetness and whiskey, at the bottom of the carton, there was this: Andy Bergheim didn't know if he was good enough.

***

Gino Swanson gestures something indecipherable toward his cohost as the camera zooms in, the music fades, and Big John Dalton squares off to the audience.

"So, we've talked about the coach, but what about the player?"

"Well, Johnny, this kid is something else. D. J. Thompson is a dual threat. His ability to scramble and buy time for his receivers is unreal. I'm telling you, Big John, this kid is the real deal all the way. He's had a phenomenal season, put up video game-like numbers, and has led The Badgers with poise and determination through every obstacle they've faced this year."

"Some say he should be in the Heisman race."

"That's the problem with playing at a school like Southwest. Even after all they've done—beating TCU in the opener, dominating their conference, racking up 38 unanswered points in the first half on a Nebraska defense that we both thought was pretty good going into that game—they still can't seem to get any respect."

"Maybe if they can pull off the bowl win people'll take'm seriously, Gino."

"Well, the Tigers had better take'm seriously because guys like D.J. Thompson make things happen. He can beat you with his legs, and he can beat you deep with his arm."

"If his arm is good to go. That was quite a hit he took in the Arizona game last week. The last I heard, his shoulder was questionable."

"You speak the truth, my friend. Those around the Badger camp are being tight lipped about his recovery, but they do seem hopeful."

"Hopeful? Is that what you're calling it? No coach. No star quarterback. The Badger faithful are down on their knees *praying* to the football gods tonight."

"More football when we return after these messages."

***

Bergheim didn't know who their sources were, but the guys at ESPN were right. The MRI was bad news. Thompson was out. It was all the coach could do to keep it under wraps until he and

Pusateri figured something out. Nothing he could do about it now. Besides, Pusateri was the real offensive mastermind. On the television, John Dalton now stood like a weather reporter dressed in a trench coat and holding an umbrella. The green screen behind him showed a montage of hurricane footage.

“When it rains it pours. At least that’s how it feels to be a Badger fan these days. It’s not looking good for Southwest: Both their coach and their star QB are looking questionable for the Pace Picante Bowl in January. Stay tuned and we’ll give you the latest.”

Bergheim turned off the TV and hefted himself off the couch. His knees creaked and felt like they could give at any second. Age is a son-of-a-bitch. Slowly, he made his way back to the kitchen, threw away the empty carton, dropped the spoon in the sink, and muddled toward the bedroom. In the morning, he’d meet with Pusateri.

***

Pusateri’s station wagon sat in the parking lot, dirt brown with three child’s seats across the back—all daughters. Coach Bergheim had already decided that if he took the job at TU, he was going to recommend the kid as his replacement. It’d be a huge opportunity for someone so young, but Pusateri could do it. He might struggle at first with the alumni politics and the Saturday morning speeches, but he’d always send the boys out with a solid game plan.

The coach parked his tiny blue Mitsubishi in his designated spot, ate another kolache, and stuffed two more into his coat pocket before fighting his way out of the car. If he took the job, he'd buy a new truck, he thought. Something easier to get in and out of. He could even buy Nancy a new car. A Jaguar. She'd like that. It was one of those things that she'd never ask him for, but he knew she'd always wanted. Bergheim gathered his notes from the backseat and headed inside to find Pusateri mapping something out on the big white board.

"Don't you ever go home, boy? No matter how early I get here, you always beat me. You tryin' steal my job?" The coach laughed.

Pusateri waited.

"So whatcha got for me, Mike? Anything good?"

Bergheim almost always called his young offensive coordinator *Mike* because he struggled with the pronunciation of his last name.

"Yeah, I'd say so, Coach. I've been watching the Arizona tapes. The meltdown in the fourth quarter wasn't McMurtry's fault. I think he can work to our advantage now that we know Thompson can't play."

"Not his fault? That boy was giving away the ball like he thought it was Christmas. Looked like he was moving in slow motion." The coach lumbered over to his desk and eased down into his chair. Lumbar support: another great creation. The Wishbone Offense, Whiskey/Ice Cream, Lumbar Support.

"No, Coach. It was our fault. More to the point, it was my fault. McMurtry and Thompson are two very different QBs."

"Well, obviously," Bergheim said.

"Look, Thompson's a speed demon. He runs hurdles. A guy like that can run the spread option and take advantage of the zone-read, but Travis McMurtry *ain't* that guy. He doesn't have that kind of speed."

"That's an understatement. The boy's got feet like a cement mixer."

"No question about that, but he does have an arm when he's got the time. And it's a pretty good one at that."

"Where are you going with this, Mike?"

"I think with a little confidence we can get him to where he's threadin' the needle on the long ball. But we can't expect him to scramble. He's corn-fed—6'5" and 255 lbs., but he's not slow. He just doesn't have quick feet. Straight ahead, if he can pick up some steam, he's a bulldozer. I'm telling you he'll be tough to bring down and can pick up tough yards."

"Jesus, I didn't realize the kid was that big." There had been a time when Andy Bergheim knew the stats of every player on his roster. These days he didn't even know most of their names.

"I'm tellin' you, the boy is a truck. He played both sides of the ball in high school and was a pretty solid linebacker on D."

"Yeah, I remember," the coach said, though in fact he didn't.

"I figure, he's built like a fullback, why not use him like one?" Pusateri found a clean spot on the white board and began to sketch out a play. "See, when Thompson gets pressure in his face, he just rolls outside the pocket and then it's a foot race—he can throw it downfield or keep it for a twenty-yard sprint up the sideline. McMurtry doesn't have that luxury. But look at this." Pusateri wiped Thompson's play from the board and drew something that looked closer to a modified wishbone. "Mac takes it in a shotgun, where the fullback would be. Then, you move the halfbacks out a bit, and keep rotating the extra receiver. If the line can give the kid just a little time, I think he can make some big plays."

"And if they blitz?" Coach leaned forward in his chair and peered over his glasses.

"Then Mac keeps it and barrels right up the middle. Like I said, he's got straight ahead speed and the Tigers love the A-gap blitz. He can split the middle all day long." Pusateri put the cap back on the dry-erase marker and waited.

"Can the boy spot it?"

"The blitz? He's got a good head on his shoulders. We just had him playing out of his element last week. The kid can do it, but it's going to take some work. And look, you can still use elements from the spread."

"Really?"

"If we can keep'm honest by establishing the ground game early, then we can start stretching out the field and testing the long ball as the game goes on." Pusateri's energy was contagious. Play after play. The man had the fire. If there was a better gameday play-caller, Bergheim had never met him.

"I like it, kid. Good ol' fashioned football—meat and potatoes. We'll punch'm in the nose and watch'm bleed." Bergheim took off his glasses and wiped the lens with his shirttail. "You're going to make a helluva fine head coach someday, Michael."

"Thanks. That means a lot coming from someone like you, Coach." He paused. "Actually, I was wanting to ask you something."

"Let me give you a piece of advice, son. Surround yourself with the best people, preferably smarter than you are. Trust me. It's gotten me this far."

The players began to arrive for their morning meetings. It was time to sell the plan. Bergheim rose from his chair and shuffled over to Pusateri.

"You wanna tell'm? They're practically yours."

"Coach, I gotta to talk to you."

"It can wait. Go fire up the troops. It's your game plan." Bergheim patted the young coach on the back and directed him toward the door.

In the meeting room, Pusateri gave his speech, drew his plays, and sold the dream that they could actually win this game no matter what, even without D.J. Thompson. He spoke with a sense of urgency. It impressed Bergheim.

"Are the rumors true about Coach?" a lineman asked.

Pusateri paused before he responded. "It doesn't matter who coaches. You're all winners. And winners win. That's what they do. That's what *you* do. WHAT DO WINNERS DO?"

"WINNERS WIN!"

"WHAT DO WINNERS DO?"

"WINNERS WIN!"

"All right, gentlemen, you have a game plan that exploits the enemy's weakness and the right quarterback to pick'm apart. Everything else is about execution. Now get out there and put this plan into motion."

"WINNERS WIN!"

***

Gino Swanson stands in front the green screen wearing a white lab coat and a stethoscope around his neck. What the audience sees behind him is a generic looking hospital background. The clicking sounds of an old telegraph machine plays through the audio.

"This just in, folks. It's official. D.J. Thompson, star quarterback for the Southwest Badgers, is a no go for the Picante Bowl." Gino bends down and disappears out of the shot. When he returns, he is wearing an oversized sombrero that teeters atop his massive head. "Four out of five doctors agree, *el elbow no bueno*. So, there you have it. The bad news for the Badgers just keeps getting worse."

The shot switches to Gino's cohost, Big John Dalton, squeezed into a track suit several sizes too small. He blows a coach's whistle in front of another green screen. This one portrays a locker room setting and looks like it may have been taken from a cheesy made-for-TV movie.

"First off, incorrect diagnosis, *señor*. The problem is Thompson's shoulder, not his elbow. I can't believe I let you operate on me."

The camera pans back across the studio, exposing the behind the scenes workings of the show. It stops on a guilty-looking Gino Sawnson, still wearing the ridiculous sombrero.

"*Ai yai yai. Lo siento, mi amigo*," Gino says, but is overcome with laughter and has to regain his composure. "Sorry, Johnny, I couldn't think of anything in Spanish that rhymed with *shoulder,* and I really wanted to wear this sweet hat."

The camera swings back to Big John and the locker room.

"I can't fault you for that, Gino. Sombreros are awesome. But what is not awesome is the Badgers' chance for victory now that Thompson is officially out."

Gino walks into John's shot, removes his sombrero, and waves it in front of Dalton like a matador taunting a bull.

"You are absolutely right, Johnny. Without Thompson, the Badgers will have to rely on their incredibly slow redshirt freshman backup, Travis McMurtry."

"Slow is right. He could make a sloth look like Walter Payton."

"Now *that's* slow."

"Stay tuned, folks. When we return, we'll take an in-depth look at Ohio State. Are they that good, or is the Big Ten *just that* bad?"

***

Pusateri spent the entire day moving kids around like chess pieces, trying to teach the new offense. Things were shaky at first, but McMurtry finally seemed to settle into a rhythm. The kid did have an arm. Coach Bergheim watched from the sidelines as Pusateri explained something to the young QB. The massive man-child nodded and returned to the huddle. The next play was a quick release up the right side to Roshawn Wallace. McMurtry looked like he was throwing darts—bullseye.

"Atta, boy," Bergheim shouted from the sideline. "That's what I wanna see."

No question that Mike Pusateri was ready for a head coaching job. The question was whether Southwest would offer it to him. Bergheim liked the idea of naming Mike as his successor and of the young coach carrying on his legacy. He just didn't trust the school's committee to make the right call. Hell, they had students on the committee. What do students know about football? They're liable to spend too much money on some washed up coach with a name when they've got the best guy for the job right under their noses.

Bergheim paced the sideline, trying to keep his mind on the scrimmage. He couldn't decide if his reasons for wanting to stay on with the Badgers until the bowl game were selfish or not. Did they really stand a better chance at beating Missouri with him at the helm instead of Mike? Probably not. And if they won without him, Mike would be set.

"As long as you've got eleven men suited up, there's always a chance," Bergheim reminded himself.

Then, like a blindside blitz to his heart, the fear rose up again. What if he took the TU job and failed? There's no room for error at a school like that. They're not a fan base known for their patience or willingness to forgive. This bowl game coming up might be his last shot as a head coach for, at least, two years, maybe more. He thought about this. How much was his legacy really worth in dollars and cents?

He forced his mind back to the field.

"Let's see what this truck of yours can do, Mike. GROUND AND POUND."

"You heard the coach, ground and pound, boys. GROUND AND POUND."

***

At the crescent-shaped desk, Big John Dalton and Gino Swanson smile as the camera zooms in and then back out.

"Just in case you've been living under some kind of giant soundproof rock this past week and haven't heard the news, the boys down at TU are trying to wrangle themselves up a new head coach. And the rumor has it that it might just be a Southwest Badger."

"Indeed, just not the one we all thought, Johnny."

Both men put their hands to their faces and do their best Macaulay Culkin *Home Alone* impressions as the camera pans in and out and in and out.

"That's right, according to the latest report from ESPN analyst Rick Ward, Coach Andy Bergheim's slow response has prompted TU to look elsewhere."

"And they're not just looking at anyone, John. Sources say they've been looking right in Bergheim's own locker room and meeting with the Badgers' offensive coordinator, Michael Pusateri."

"And that's bad news for the Badgers."

They repeat the Macaulay Culkin scream.

"You've got that right, buddy. Let's be honest, Pusateri is the real whiz kid behind all that Badger magic we've seen this year. He's the puppet master. *The Geppetto of the offense*."

"And now TU's gone and tried to poach him right out from under Coach Bergheim's nose. Gino, do I smell foul play?"

"I'm tellin' you, Johnny, I think that Andy Bergheim's reluctance to leave his Badger faithful on the cusp of their first ever bowl game is admirable."

"Bros before hoes, right, Gino?" Big John goes for the fist-bump but is shunned by his partner.

"Remember, ladies, be sure to send your complaints *to ESPN—care of Big John Dalton.*" Gino smiles at the camera. "But seriously, Andy Bergheim has made a commitment to his Badgers. I respect that. Unfortunately, it appears this decision has rubbed the big dogs at TU the wrong way."

"A little baby powder helps with chafing, I've found."

"Way too much information, Johnny," Gino says, throwing his crimson handkerchief up in the air like a penalty flag.

"I gotta say, Gino, I don't understand this move by TU. What are they thinking? Spite is seldom a good reason to hire a football coach." He slaps the desktop for emphasis.

"I think they're thinking that if they can't have Bergheim, then they'll take the next best thing."

Big John looks puzzled. "When did TU become the ugly girl willing to dance with every pimple faced kid that asks her?"

"I think it was when she went 3 and 9 last season. And let's not kid ourselves, Bergheim is still the first choice as far as we know, but Pusateri ain't no slouch either."

"That may be true, but is he ready? I mean, I've still got questions about whether or not Bergheim is ready, much less this Pusateri kid."

"Come on, John. You don't think *anybody* is ready to take the TU job. At a certain point, football is just football. Xs and Os. And these two coaches both know football."

"But do they know TU football? That's the question."

"You're killing me, Johnny." Gino spins his chair one full rotation and addresses the camera.

"We've got to take a quick commercial break and pay some bills. Meanwhile, my cohost here is going to try and raise the spirits of Bear Bryant and Knute Rockne from the dead in the hope that one of them might actually be *ready* for the TU job."

"*Now* we're talking, Gino."

***

After practice, and after most of the players had cleared out, Andy Bergheim pulled the bottle from his file cabinet and poured himself a glass, squirted a splash from his water bottle and took a sip. He was pretty sure he'd made up his mind.

"You got enough for me, boss?"

"Mike, my boy. Come on in." He poured the young coach a healthy one. "So, how good do you really think we're gonna be? 'Cause I gotta say we started looking all right out there." He leaned back in his chair and waited to hear what he wanted to hear.

"I think these kids can run with anybody in the country, Coach, but it's gonna take some time and a lot of work. A lot of work." Pusateri took a sip. "Coach, you've got to take a personal interest in McMurtry. You've got to build his confidence—work with him one on one. You've forgotten more about the wishbone than I've ever known, and that's basically what you'll be running."

"Yep, brilliant, son. I love it. We'll beat'm down and make'm breathe heavy. Just run it up their throats. I love it. You're going to take this team to new levels, Mike."

"That's what I wanted to talk to you about, Coach." He paused. "TU offered me the job last night. Jack Spencer called me around 8:30. We talked for about an hour."

Bergheim reached for his whiskey, his goddamn hand shaking from the punch to the gut. He sipped. "I don't understand."

"The alumni's hot for a change. They say it's my offense they want. They don't care who runs it."

He took another sip of whiskey. "Are you sure? They might be trying to tighten the screws on me. These negotiations are ruthless."

"I don't think so, Coach."

Bergheim shifted in his chair, took another drink, and composed himself. The bastards were trying to tighten the screws.

"Did you talk money?"

"Yes, sir. Nothing's set in stone. Just some numbers thrown around."

"Big numbers?"

"Bigger than I've ever seen."

"I bet." Bergheim nodded, drained his drink, and poured another. "Well, if they're talking numbers, it sounds like they're pretty serious. This could be big for you and the girls, Mike."

"That's why I came up here last night."

"You were here all night?"

"Well, I wasn't going to leave you guys without a plan. I had to come up with something in case I took the job. I mean I—I couldn't completely abandon y'all, not in good conscience."

"No, I appreciate that. You're a better man than most." He offered the bottle. "Top you off?"

"Please." Pusateri's glass met Bergheim halfway. "You're not mad, Coach?"

"Mike, do you know what's really amazing?"

"What, Coach?"

"Whiskey/Ice Cream. Ever had it? It's one of the greatest creations of all time. Stumbled upon it last night. You should try it." The coach smiled and Pusateri looked confused. "You just pour it right on top. It's real easy."

"Sure, Coach."

"You see, Mike, sometimes in this life good things land right in your lap. And with good recruiting that *sometimes* starts to happen a lot more often." He hesitated and then continued. "My advice for you is don't let'm pressure you. This is the single biggest decision of your life. This is your career."

"I know, Coach."

"Take tonight and think about it. Think long and hard. Is this really the right move for you at this point in your career? TU fans are brutal. If you don't produce, they'll bury you with Jimmy Hoffa. Make a list of all the pros and cons. Talk it over with your wife. Sleep on it. Make damn sure it's the right move. You're young. You don't have to rush anything."

"And if I still decide it's the right thing to do?"

"Then take the job, Mike. Take it for you. Take it for your family. But remember, it's not just about the money. You'll probably hardly ever see your family once you start. You're going to have to get your ass out there on the road and start recruiting as soon as possible, talking to the players and their parents. It's going to be a full-time job to turn that program around. It's a damn mess out there."

"And the Badgers?"

"Don't worry about them. They're good goddamn boys. We've got a game plan, and now we just have to execute." Bergheim raised his glass.

"Thanks, Coach."

***

Big John Dalton and Gino Swanson play some variation of patty-cake as the theme music comes to a close. They turn and act as if they are embarrassed to have been caught.

"According to our ESPN's own Rick Ward, the word on the street is that Southwest coach Andy Bergheim has elected to stay with his team and coach the Badgers in their first ever bowl appearance—renewing his contract for five more years."

"That's just the kind of guy he is. Team all the way."

"Unfortunately, Bergheim is going to have to try and pull it off without the help of the offensive genius that is Coach Mike Pusateri, who is rumored to have accepted the TU job."

"It's a huge loss for the Badgers."

"First they lose Thompson. Now they lose Pusateri—the master of the hybrid spread option offense. Can they recover and show up ready to compete against the Tigers in January?"

"With Andy Bergheim calling the plays, I'm sure Southwest will come ready to play. His teams play hardnosed football and they always show up."

"Well, we'll see January third. And when we come back, we'll explore Bama's big D in detail."

"The thing about Bama's defense is that they play great defense."

"That makes absolutely no sense, Gino, but we'll discuss it anyway when we get back from these words from our sponsors."

***

Andy Bergheim's new favorite flavor of Whiskey/Ice Cream was English Toffee Caramel. The crispy chocolate covered toffee was a nice change. It added that something special. An hour earlier, David Carroll, the president of the university, had called to say that Southwest was willing to discuss renewing his contract a year early, and for a lot more money. It was the smart play for everyone. Bergheim could buy that truck after all. And something nice for Nancy, too. Not a Jaguar but something nice. He looked at his watch. She was probably in good spirits this evening, wrapping things up at her weekly *Paint by the Glass* class, which she taught at the wine bar a few blocks from the campus. His phone rested on the coffee table where he'd left it after the call from Carroll. Bergheim sat for a moment churning the ice-cream round and round. He loved how the texture complimented the taste, that smooth whiskey sweetness, those bits of candy hidden deep in the creamy cold. His heart pounded mildly. He thought about Pusateri and his three girls, but only for a second. He thought of his players, all good kids. Then he picked up the phone, scrolled through his contacts, and placed the call to Jack Spencer at TU.

"Hello, Jack," he said. "It's Andy. Is it too late?"

THE EXPERIMENT

It was as if Caesar's Palace had joined forces with Fisher-Price to create the ultimate in toddler gaming, Tori thought. *My First Little Casino* hummed under the florescent lights inside the otherwise nondescript flat-white lab room. Tiny but brightly colored slot machines and roulette wheels covered in Sesame Street stickers surrounded the little moon-shaped tables where the card games would be played.

"So, I'm a blackjack dealer?"

"More or less," said Dr. Pearce. "First, you will teach them the system and the corresponding strategies. Then, you will deal blackjack while they practice what they've learned and we observe their behavior."

The psychologist, a tall bearded man, easily six-seven, maybe more, towered over Tori's petite frame. It was a little intimidating. She could only imagine how he made the children feel—looming over them and scribbling in his notebook.

Tori had signed up for the experiment without knowing what it was all about. All she knew was that it had something to do with kids, would look good on a resume, and paid well. Nineteen hundred dollars to be exact—a little more than half of what she currently owed the university for spring tuition. She was so close to graduating, and she'd already sold off her car and everything else of value that she owned in order to pay for her previous semesters and living expenses. Reaching out to her parents was out of the question. They were part of the problem. Her father was sick and in some serious financial trouble. Her mother filing for divorce made things worse. It was so selfish the way her mother abandoned him at his lowest point—leaving him dangling there to be picked apart by the hovering vultures—the banks, the credit cards, the casinos. *The fucking casinos.*

As a former investment banker, her father was a gambler by trade. Risk and reward—his life's blood. And if he'd had the money, he would've paid her tuition no questions asked. But he didn't, and to make matters worse, his money troubles had become Tori's. He had borrowed against her name in order to invest in a string of strip malls that went belly-up before ground was ever broken and now even student loans were no longer an option for Tori. Her credit was as bad as his. Now the short, fat, red-faced man camped out on Tori's secondhand couch, had been there since her mother had thrown him out over eight months ago. Broke, unemployed, unhireable, and in desperate need of a brain surgery he couldn't afford, even if he still had health insurance.

To the casinos, her father was an easy mark. It was not uncommon for him to receive calls, letters, and brochures from the various hosts around the country trying to entice him back through their doors. The calls Tori could do nothing about, but she always tried to intercept the mail before he got a chance to see what they were offering. And they were always offering something.

"Come on, it's Eddie Money," he'd tell her. "'Two Tickets to Paradise,' you love that song, and it's free. We'll make a father-daughter weekend of it."

"It's not free, Dad. You and I both know that they only want you there so you'll gamble. Haven't you given them enough already?"

Her father would slump, defeated, and nod like a scolded child. It was as if he had to be reminded each time that he had a problem and that the casinos were just trying to exploit him. Tori knew he was helpless, and she did everything she could to protect him.

Now, as Dr. Pearce led her past the craps tables in the laboratory, she asked,

"Isn't all this a bit advanced for kids this age? I mean, what's the point?"

"We're studying the effects of gambling on the brain—games of chance. You see, these kinds of goal-related stimuli cause the blood flow to the brain to change in ways not unlike that seen in those taking euphoria-inducing drugs. It's what causes the addiction."

Tori knew all about this. Despite whatever her mother said, her father wasn't a bad man, just an addict with a brain tumor.

"So, like neurons and stuff," she said, "like how the ones in the reward-seeking part of the brain can override a person's rationale and that sort of thing?" she asked.

"Basically," he said, and turned away as if the conversation was over.

"But why kids?" she asked, curiosity getting the best of her. "And why are we teaching them to cheat?"

"Card counting is *not* cheating. It's frowned upon, but it's not illegal or even against the rules. It's merely a way that the player might shift the odds away from the house and into his or her favor." He stopped abruptly and turned to her. "I'm sorry, Miss.... What was your name?"

"Tori. Tori Martin."

Afraid she'd stepped over the line, Tori reached her hand out to make the introduction official, but he let it hang there, awkwardly, until she drew it back. He cleared his throat.

"Yes, Miss Martin," he said. "I believe your job is to work with the children, deal blackjack, and supervise them during said activity. Why don't you leave the details of the experiment to my colleagues and I?"

"Colleagues and me," she said.

"Excuse me?"

"Nothing."

***

"It's not fair. Why can't you help me?" she asked her mother one evening over the phone. "I can't afford him."

"Honey, I have my own bills to pay. And, believe me, lawyers aren't cheap. They bill by the hour, you know."

"He has a brain tumor. It's not like all that erratic behavior was really him."

"That doesn't excuse anything."

"You heard Dr. Grossman. The tumor is pushing on his brain and disrupting his filters. He can't help himself. He doesn't know what's right or wrong."

"And that's my problem? I haven't been in love with your father for a very long time—way before any of this started. Sometimes I wonder if I ever loved him." Tori's mother paused for what seemed like an excessive amount of time before letting out a long, dramatic sigh and continued. "You're a big girl now. It's time you start figuring these things out on your own. You can't be dependent on others for the rest of your life, Victoria. Why do you think I went back to work as soon as you were old enough to drive?"

Tori had heard this speech before. It was well-rehearsed, and she could even tell where her mother had refined certain parts, perfecting her delivery.

"I don't know, probably because you were already planning on leaving Dad. Or, was it because you wanted to fuck your new boss, Mark Hadlow?" Tori heard her mother scoff on the other end of the line. "Oh, I'm sorry. Did I offend you? I just can't remember which came first. Remind me again how all that went down?"

Again, her mother paused and the silence felt thick and heavy. Tori knew she wasn't helping her case, but she was so angry she couldn't keep the words from coming out of her mouth.

"I won't have you speak to me this way. I feel bad for your father. I do. But I will not let his problems ruin my life. This is not what I signed up for."

"Not what you signed up for? *To have and to hold, till death do you part.* It's exactly what you signed up for. Don't you see that? God, you're such a fucking hypocrite."

"Maybe when you get older, you'll understand," her mother said, and ended the call.

Her mother's words lingered as the line went dead. Her voice cold enough to give Tori chills. Her entire life had been a lie—every birthday, every holiday, every second of every day.

***

Counting cards is easy. A six-year-old can do it. This is because they're not really counting cards. They're just keeping a running tally of what's been dealt and assigning a value. It's called the *Hi-Lo Method.* Cards two through six are given the point value of positive one, seven through nine equal zero, and tens, face cards, and aces all get assigned a negative one. As the cards are dealt, the counter either adds or subtracts one to the overall running tally, or true count, unless the card dealt is a seven, eight, or nine, then the counter leaves the total tally alone. The higher the count, the more face cards there are still floating in the deck. That's it. That's all there is to it—mostly. There's also a lot of strategy involved. This is where the six-year-olds struggle.

The children in Tori's group were chosen because they excelled at basic math. It was Tori's job to teach them blackjack, which turned out to be easier said than done. Blackjack at its root is a simple game—get as close to twenty-one as you can without going over. But Dr. Pearce and his crew were not pushing the standard hit on sixteen, stand on seventeen kind of game Tori remembered her father teaching her as a child. Pearce's strategy was much more complex. Tori had to learn the material herself before she could even begin to devise a lesson plan that the children could follow. She'd been given charts that illustrated things like pair splitting and what to do with various hard and soft totals. She didn't know what any of it meant and was afraid to admit she was in over her head. She needed this money. At the end of her second day, she knew she had to ask for help. That evening, after clearing all the plates from the dinner table, against her better judgment, she spoke to her father.

"Oh, honey, blackjack's my game," he told her. "Always has been."

"Dad, *we're* not playing blackjack. I just have to teach these kids about all this stuff. Come on, focus. What's a soft total?"

"Whether a hand is hard or soft depends on the ace and its flexibility. Soft just means that the hand is flexible." He dealt a two, a four, and an ace out on the coffee table to demonstrate. "Now, see, that there's a soft seventeen. Do you know why?"

Tori shook her head. She noticed her father's right knee was bouncing like a crackhead's on a cop show.

"Because the ace can be a one or an eleven, so really we've got a choice between seven and seventeen. In other words, if we hit, we don't have to worry about busting because we can just call the ace a one and go from there. Is this making any sense?"

"Yeah, I think so." Tori pieced it together in her head. "And a hard hand just means that the cards are what they are, right?"

"Exactly."

He then taught her how to split pairs and the theory behind it, and together they developed a color-coded learning block system for teaching the children the various strategic charts on betting. After a while, Tori began to yawn.

"Jesus, it's almost three," she said. "I've gotta get some sleep."

"Don't you wanna play a few hands before you call it a night? You know, try it out?"

"No. I'm going to bed and you should too."

"I'm not really that tired," he said, and began shuffling the cards—his knee still bouncing.

"Go to bed, Dad."

***

Over the days that followed, Tori found herself surprised by how quickly the kids caught on. Their natural competitive spirits fueled their desire to learn, and before long they were ready to play actual hands using candy and treats as poker chips. And the better they got, the better she got. It was fun. She even downloaded a blackjack app to her phone and counted cards in much the same way that most girls her age played *Words with Friends*. It was easy to see how people got addicted, and she wondered about the long- term effects on the children.

One afternoon, a few weeks into the experiment, as Tori dealt out several hands to her tiny gamblers, she could feel Dr. Pearce standing behind her. Between hands, she stole a glance over her right shoulder. He smiled and gave a quick nod. Tori returned the smile and continued to deal.

When she was relieved an hour later, Dr. Pearce cornered her by the snack machine in the break room.

"Miss Martin, correct?"

"Yes, sir."

He peered at her over the top of his wire-rimmed glasses and began to scratch his beard. The room was so white, so bright, that Tori could see the specks of dandruff gently floating down from his chin. It reminded her of an Eiffel Tower snow globe she'd received one Christmas as a child. Or was it the Empire State Building?

"You're making excellent progress with your group," he said. "They're two stages ahead of where we expected them to be by now and three stages ahead of any of the other groups. You seem to have quite the knack for this."

Tori shrugged. "I guess. I still don't understand what it is we're doing here."

"I assure you that these children are well-taken care of, Miss Martin. In fact, they're paid much more handsomely than you'll be, if that makes a difference."

"I just don't see the point."

"I hate to keep coming back to this, but it's not your job to see the point. Do you understand?"

Tori said nothing. Instead, she tilted her head and looked curiously up at the giant man in the lab coat.

He continued. "Please know that we have the children's best interests at heart and that during the experiment they'll be learning valuable cognitive skills that will surely benefit each and every one of them as they go on in life."

Tori nodded as if she understood. His speech sounded like one of her mother's rehearsed responses, but she reminded herself not to push her luck. She needed the money, and so she let it go. After all, they weren't her children.

***

By the time the check from the experiment arrived, the university had already begun adding late fees to Tori's outstanding balance. The nineteen-hundred would barely make a dent, but it would keep her from getting dropped.

"And it's not just that," she told her mother. "I have to pay rent. I have to pay bills. What the hell am I going to do?"

"Of course, your father can't help at all, can he? He's such a sponge," her mother said in that know-it-all way she had.

"Mom, don't start. He's doing better. The therapy and the meds are helping."

"Sure they are."

"They are. Why do you have to always be like this?"

"A temporary fix, Tori. That's all. He can't be trusted. Don't fool yourself."

"I know. And if he doesn't get the surgery, he'll die anyways." Tori paused to get her breath. "Of course, you don't care about that, do you?"

"That's not fair. I have my own life to live."

"Whatever," Tori said, ending the call in a huff.

***

Two weeks later, Tori opened a letter addressed to her father from the Eldorado congratulating him on his "recent success." She felt like she was going to explode.

"What's this?" she asked.

"I've been meaning to tell you about that," her father said.

"And?"

"I promise I haven't been gambling."

"Really? 'Cause that's not what it says right here." She held the letter within a few inches of his face and pointed at the text.

"I know, right? I've been on a streak. But that's the thing. I'm not gambling." He walked to the couch and unzipped one of the back cushions and pulled out a large wad of bills. He held it up and handed it all to Tori. "There should be enough for rent and bills there, maybe even a little left over for school."

"I don't understand." She stood frozen, staring at the money in one hand and holding the letter in the other.

"You know what? I'm glad this happened. I've been trying to figure out how to tell you, honey." He became excited, pacing as he spoke. "I've been using your system. It works. It really works. I mean, I've known about card counting my whole life, but I never took the time to learn it."

"How long has this been going on?"

"I've only tried it on a small scale. You know, taking a quick day-trip on the Greyhound over to Shreveport on the days when I knew you were working late. I just play the five-dollar hands—nothing big."

"I can't believe you're counting cards."

"Yeah, but it's not *really* gambling."

Tori stared at her father. He spoke like a man who'd been saved by Jesus himself. It was clear he believed every word he said.

"I mean, the reason blackjack is so popular is because it's the only game where the odds of the house are about even with that of the player's. And when I know the count, then it's like *I'm* the house. The odds are in my favor."

"It's still gambling."

"Technically, yeah, but the odds are in my favor, so it's just barely gambling."

Tori ran her fingers through her hair and tried to think of what to say.

"You know, together, we could really clean house," he told her.

"Jesus, Dad. How can you say that?"

"I'm just sayin'. Think about it, hon'. I know you've been playing blackjack on your phone. Heck,

I bet you're better at it than I am by now. The two of us, we could turn things around."

"Dad," she said. "It's not right."

"Not right?" He threw up his hands. "Look at that money in your hand. That's *our* money. I took it back from the casinos. They took it from me, and I took it back."

"I don't know what to say to you right now." Tori stared at the money and sighed.

"Tell me you're in," he said.

She looked up at him and felt like she might cry. Her grip tightened on the wad of cash.

"Think about it," he said. "One weekend and we can make enough to pay off your tuition and then some. A few more weekends and maybe we can start saving towards my surgery. We'll never know, Tori, if we don't try." His eyes were beady with intensity. They dug inside of her. He pointed at the letter in her other hand. "What are they offering?"

"Two nights and fifteen hundred in chips."

He smiled. "I think God's trying to tell us something." He pressed his hands together as if to pray.

"I seriously doubt it's God," she said.

***

They hardly spoke a word on the bus. Tori tried to sleep but her father's excitement—his vibrating knee, his incessant finger-tapping—made it impossible. She pulled out her phone and began to practice in silence while the bus droned on toward Shreveport.

At the casino, a few hours later, Tori saw a familiar look on her father's face. It was the look she herself had in that old picture from Disney World, when she was eight and got to meet Mickey Mouse. Her eyes were glassy with wonderment, just like his now. It made her uneasy.

"Snap out of it, or we turn around right now," she told him.

Her father nodded and took a deep breath.

"Are you good?" she asked.

"Yeah, I'm ready. Let's do this."

As they walked through the brash lobby, Tori couldn't help but think of that scene from *Rainman* where Tom Cruise and Dustin Hoffman walk through the casino in their matching suits. She looked over at her rainman and shook her head. She grabbed his arm when they reached the floor and led the way over the red carpet.

The place was brighter than she'd expected, almost as bright as Pearce's lab but not as florescent. The ceilings were high and the chandeliers were practically stacked on top of each other across it. Even the room's support columns lit up at the top. It was as if they'd stuck a bulb into every space they could fit one.

"If awfully bright in here, isn't it?"

"That's so you don't get sleepy."

"Of course it is," she said. Then she stopped and turned to her father, squaring him at the shoulders. "Blackjack, nothing else. Remember?"

"Tori, I'm not a damn child."

She gave him a look that, she believed, said everything—but just in case, she reiterated: "No roulette, no craps, no Texas Hold'em, and absolutely no slots."

"You don't have to remind me. I'm only playing the sure thing from now on, sweetie. I promise."

"All right," she said, walking again. "Let's get the chips."

***

Playing at a real table with real competition and a real dealer rattled her. This was where the big kids played. Big Bird and Snuffleupagus were nowhere to be found. She struggled to think, much less count or bet properly. She quickly lost two hundred, excused herself from the table, and walked over to where her father was playing. A small crowd had begun to form around him. He was in the zone and people love a winner. Tori tried to get his attention but had no luck. She headed to the bar instead, hoping to settle her nerves with a few stiff drinks.

By the time she returned, a few casino employees and a large man she assumed to be the pit boss had taken an interest in her father's skill. With each hand he won, the men grew closer. Tori's heart raced. She tried to catch his attention without being too obvious, but he never looked in her direction. She pushed her way through the crowd, but just as she reached her father, he excused himself from the game and took his winnings with him.

He smiled and winked as he brushed by her and whispered, "Not a bad start. I think I'll take a break and see to our accommodations."

Tori nodded and took a moment before making her way to another table. This time she chose the one with the oldest, most gentle looking grandfather type dealer. She looked back to see if she could find her father, but he was gone.

Again, she started off rough, losing the first few hands and stumbling over her words when she tried to say *hit* or *stand*. And then it happened. Blackjack. She started playing multiple hands, doubling down, and splitting her pairs just as she'd taught the children to do. And as her true count rose, so did her bets and vice versa. She barely noticed that her father had come back down to the gaming floor. She saw him briefly, watching her play, but she was afraid she might lose her concentration and returned her focus to the game—to the count. The next time she looked up, he was nowhere to be seen.

Tori's success had begun to draw some attention from a few of the casino staff, but she was so close to her goal of five thousand dollars. Rather than walking away like her father had done, she chose to fake a minor slump until the crowd began to lose interest. She lost a few hands outright and surrendered a few others. She played up her *I'm just a cute college girl having fun* persona and flirted with the men around her. And as soon as she felt it was safe again, she began to rebuild her fortune.

Hours went by, hand after hand, table after table, and Tori rode the streak—knowing when to let off the throttle and when to go for the throat. She was surrounded by a small kingdom of multi-colored chips when she decided it was time to call it a night. The deck steamed it was so hot, overflowing with high cards, but she reminded herself not to get greedy. *One more hand*, she told herself. *One more hand and I'm done.*

When the dealer called for bets, Tori anted up the table's maximum of four hundred dollars. The dealer then made his rounds, presenting Tori with a ten of spades and a queen of diamonds—two tens. She split the pair and doubled down, an unusual deviation for anyone not counting cards, but no one seemed to notice. No one except the dealer, who shot her a curious look. She smiled and gave a slight shrug. He returned the gesture and continued dealing. Tori's next card was an ace—*BLACKJACK.*

"YES!" she screamed, jumping up and down.

The people around her cheered. Strangers congratulated her.

"Whoa! Look at that, boys. That's all she wrote for this ol' gal. I think I'm gonna stop while I'm ahead," she said, and began gathering up her winnings. She tipped the dealer several hundred and snuck off through the crowd to cash in. On her way, she passed her father at the five-dollar slots, drinking a scotch and feeding bills into the machine. He reminded her of the children from Pearce's experiment, hunched over, eyes glued to the screen.

"What are you doing?" she asked.

"I got banned from the tables."

"But why are you at the slots. We had a deal."

"I know, honey, I tried waiting for you." He hung his head and looked pathetic. "I guess I figured five dollars at a time's better than losing it all on one game of craps."

"How much have you lost?"

"Maybe five or six hundred?"

"Jesus, Dad. How much do you still have?"

He smiled up at her. "A couple thousand easy. You?"

"A little over ten," she said.

Her father's face lit up. He jumped to his feet and threw his arms around her. She stiffened and pulled away, careful not to spill her tray of chips.

"What's wrong?" he asked. "Aren't you happy?"

"I'm not sure."

They cashed in her chips, and she made her father hand over his winnings as well before heading upstairs to their suite.

"Wait till you see this place, honey, it's gonna blow your mind. There's a flat-screen and a jacuzzi in every room," he said as he swiped the room key and the light blinked green.

"Good, I could use a bath."

"It takes a lot out of you, doesn't it? Anyone who thinks it isn't work has never tried it."

She turned and faced her father, looking him in the eye. "Can I trust you if I take a bath? Will you promise me you'll stay here in the room?"

"Of course, sweetie. I'm not *that* bad, am I?"

"Dad, we both know you are. This was a one-time thing. We're not doing this again. Do you understand?"

"Well, we're certainly not doing it again here," he said. "They'll probably never have us back."

"That's not what I meant and you know it."

"I know." He sat on the couch, his knee bouncing. "I guess I got caught up in the moment is all."

"That's the problem. You always do."

He nodded. "Why don't you pour yourself a glass of wine and draw yourself a nice warm bath? I'll order us up some room service—filet mignon for my little girl." He smiled.

"That sounds good, but I think I'll have the salmon—something light." She walked to the bar and grabbed the complimentary bottle of merlot, the corkscrew, and a wine glass.

"Sure. Whatever you want," he said.

"Thanks, Daddy."

She made her way into her room and shut the door behind her. It really was nice—amazing, even. The bathroom was almost bigger than her entire apartment, and the low-hanging glass chandelier danced and sparkled in the reflection off the mirror. She turned the water on and adjusted the temperature until it felt right, and then plugged the tub and began to undress. She opened the wine and poured a tall glass as the water began to rise. She wrapped herself in a robe that hung from the door and went back to check on her father. He was on the phone ordering their dinner and joking with the person on the other end. He looked happy, almost playful, and when he saw her standing there, his smile widened. She tried to smile back but couldn't. All she could think about were her mother's words: *Don't fool yourself. He can't be trusted.* Her heart sank. She took a deep breath, exhaled slowly, quietly closed the door, and began to cry.

THE LAST DROP

Robert Lee

Barbara Halyard sat one early evening in her recliner by the window plodding through another book of crosswords her daughter, Carol, had sent in her last care-package from Abilene. It was the kind you see on display at the supermarket checkout counter next to the tabloids and crock-pot recipes—an impulse buy, as they say. She imagined Carol fumbling through her purse for her billfold and coupons as the kids tried to sneak candy and toys into the cart. Perhaps while slapping a Snickers out of little Billy's hand, the book of crosswords caught Carol's eye and she thought of *dear old Mom*.

The evening news rattled on in the background and an obese cat named Shelby slept in her lap. After throwing in the towel on twenty-seven across, Barbara set the book on top of the morning's issue of the *San Angelo Standard-Times*, which she subscribed to now because the *Robert Lee Observer* refused to deliver anymore. When she called to complain, the woman on the other end told her she could find everything online.

"Excuse me?" Barbara had asked.

"On the internet. It's all there. You just subscribe and fill out the credit card info and you'll have access to the entire paper. It's quite simple."

"But there's no paper? Is this one of those computer things like the Facebook and the Twitter?"

The woman giggled. "Um, yes, ma'am. Do you have a computer?"

"My daughter and her husband gave me one a few years ago, but I've never been able to get the hang of it. The grandkids play on it when they visit, but mostly it just sits there," Barbara explained. "And I don't give my credit card to anyone."

"That's good, ma'am, but it's all very secure."

"Sounds fishy to me. A newspaper that's not even really a paper? I try to stay informed, and I know all about how the internet scams people, especially people my age."

"It's true. You really have to be careful. But I assure you that you don't need to worry about our site."

"Nah, I'm not interested in all that. I'll just have to read somebody else's paper, I guess."

And so she did. In fact, she subscribed to every paper available in the area and read every single one each day. Besides the obituaries and gardening section, she loved the human interest stories about the drought. She liked to imagine people's lives and the troubles they faced. It scared her, but that made it more interesting.

***

Medina Lake

T-Roy Liddell's fat feet poured over his flip-flops as he made his way across the jagged earth. The newspaper man from San Antonio followed close behind, commenting on the "labyrinth of mini-canyons" and "gelatinous muck" that the dry lakebed had left exposed. These *mini-canyons* had to be at least three or four feet deep and some a foot wide, if not more. Bluebonnets flourished where boats had once been docked. Piers led nowhere but to grassy fields. Charlie Whitson's old Bumble Bee bass boat sat about a hundred yards out in the exact same spot where it'd sunk some fifteen years earlier. T-Roy had been thinking about trying to salvage the boat but hadn't gotten around to it just yet. He doubted there's any hope for the Johnson outboard motor still mounted on the backside, but you never know and these were desperate times. The ever-receding waters had uncovered all kinds of trash and treasures, such as a Jeep Wrangler and a few hot tubs and endless amounts of abandoned lawn furniture. T-Roy understood the boat, but some of these other items baffled him. How does somebody drown a Jeep?

"It's the worst I've ever seen," he told the young Mexican reporter. The kid looked like a college boy from a movie in his khaki slacks, brand new Timberland boots, and light blue Polo golf shirt. T-Roy adjusted his overalls around his gut. "Of course, I wasn't around in the 50s."

"And how is this drought affecting your business, Mr. Liddell?"

"I run a bait and tackle shop on a lake that don't have any water in it. How the hell do you think it's affecting my business, son?"

"I guess that was a stupid question."

"Damn right it was." T-Roy spat a stream of dip-spit that caught the wind and flew a good seven or eight feet before reaching the peak of its arch and falling, ultimately disappearing into one of the many crevasses that spider webbed around them. "I mean they only got one public boat ramp left open. The damn lake's nearing a hundred feet low." He spit again. "And the less water we got, the less fish we got. I was talking to my buddy at the Parks and Wildlife Department, and he told me the last fish survey they did said the bass population's less than a fifth of what it was five years ago. A fifth. Nobody's buying nightcrawlers for fish that ain't there."

"What about the catfish?" the young man asked.

"Shit, they're more resourceful, but they're getting so hungry they'll bite at a bare hook." He hesitated and took in his surroundings, running his thumbs behind the suspenders of his overalls. "Yep, it's dryer than a goddamn Baptist wedding 'round here. I'll be honest, I don't think we're gonna make it through another year like this last one. About to pack it in, I tell you what."

"I heard from somebody in town that there's an old Mormon settlement that'll soon be visible if this drought keeps up."

"Yeah, I reckon it will, but don't go expecting much. I knew some folks that explored it back in the 90s with a bunch of scuba gear. They said it's nothing but the old foundations, no actual buildings or anything."

"Still, it's kind of cool," the reporter said.

"I guess if you're into that sort of thing. Me, I prefer to pay my mortgage."

"Well, of course. I didn't mean…." The reporter regrouped and changed gears. "I heard that when the lake does refill, that all the grass and shrubs growing along the shores here will make for great fish habitat and that the population will come back better than ever."

"I suppose it will. And won't that be fortunate for whoever picks my place up out of foreclosure? Lucky devils." T-Roy turned to face the young man, bent at the waist, and spit between the cracks that separated them. "Let me tell you something, son. This lake ain't just about fishing and water skiing. It's about life. This lake used to irrigate the farms around Castroville and provide drinking water for the people on the south side of San Antonio." He paused a moment. "We're in survival mode here, so pardon me if I struggle to find the bright side of all this. Our goddamn way of living is dryin' up. Our next wars will be over water." He shook his head and spit a direct shot onto one of the reporter's boots. "Mark my words, boy. Water wars," he said as he cleared his throat and spat on the other boot. "By the way, I think you got some of that *gelatinous muck* on your fancy new shoes."

***

Robert Lee

As the TV transitioned from commercials back to the news, it caught Barbara's attention when she heard the anchorman mention the E.V. Spence Reservoir, the town's only source of drinking water. Triple-digit days and the absolute absence of rain had dried everything up. The reservoir was "more than ninety-nine percent empty," according to the man with an ethnic name, deep voice, and slicked back hair. Efforts to drill municipal water wells had been less than successful so far, as the water often proved to be tainted by improperly capped oil wells that had been long since abandoned. The newest plan on the books was to dig a small, but deep, holding pond near the water plant with what was left in the lake—the idea being that the pond would be "less vulnerable to evaporation and algae growth than Spence." Best case scenario, once full, it would provide the town of Robert Lee with water "through April."

The news then began showing pictures of upscale lake homes that were no longer on a lake. The majority of them had been abandoned by their owners, family photos still hanging on the walls. The public pool was nothing more than a large cement hole. Cattle lay dead in the fields. Some dehydrated. Some poisoned by the hydrocyanic acid found in the stressed-out Johnson grass they were left to eat. Businesses closed. Pets and livestock were abandoned and forced to fend for themselves. The idea of turning on the faucet and nothing coming out kept small children awake at night. Carol begged her mother to come live with her in Abilene, but Barbara couldn't imagine living anywhere else. Her daughter called her stubborn, but really, she was afraid. Her friends were here, her church, her life. Her parents, two siblings, and her George all rested just beyond the rusty-white pole sign that read: ROBERT LEE

CEMETERY. She found comfort in this, but she didn't know why.

***

San Saba

Besides shaving their heads in an act of support and solidarity with their mother, Janice Pawlik's two teenage daughters had also pooled their money together and bought Janice a miniature donkey in the hopes of raising her spirits during her first battle with cancer. At the time, they didn't know donkeys were *companion animals* and needed fellow jacks in order to fight the loneliness. This is how the obsession began. Janice lost both breasts. Now, seventeen years and twenty-seven donkeys later, the daughters, Paige and Katy, have moved off and started families of their own. Meanwhile, Eeyore became the elder statesman of the Pawlik's small ranch outside of town. Often shadowed by his redheaded pigmy partner in crime, Señor Enchi, the much greyer Eeyore barreled through the house with a *get-out-of-my-way* attitude like he owned the place. He was an affectionate animal, though not particularly polite. The rest of the donkeys were full-sized and not allowed in the house. This is where Martin drew the line.

"We can't afford the ones we have, Janice. You're going to have to learn to turn a few away," he told his wife. Martin was six and a half years younger than Janice, but the years were beginning to take their toll on him as well. The depth of his crow's feet told the story of a man who had spent his entire life working in the sun. His bones creaked like an old house settling in the night. "Unless the Foundation is willing to foot the bill, I don't see how we can take on another one."

Janice turned her head, refusing to look at her husband. She knew he was right. The drought showed no signs of letting up and the cost of hay had more than doubled from last year and was still climbing. More horses and donkeys were being abandoned along the state's highways every day. Law enforcement and rescue organizations scrambled to find each orphan a home. Smaller and far less practical than horses, donkeys are not near as valuable. Hardly any of the auction barns would even waste their time putting one on the block. Adoption was rare. Janice felt she was their only hope.

"It's just that, from the picture, he looks like the spitting image of Eeyore, only bigger."

"Jesus, Janice, he's a donkey. They all look alike."

"Watch your mouth. He'll hear you," she said, knowing full-well how ridiculous she sounded. Miniature donkeys have an average lifespan of around thirty years and full-sized donkeys generally make it to at least thirty-five, so it's not uncommon for their owners to become quite attached. Janice lit a cigarette in defiance, a forty-six-year-old habit. She found some strange satisfaction in the fact that it wouldn't be lung cancer or even her breasts that would do her in.

Her leathery skin tone hid the early signs until she finally noticed the yellowing in her eyes about a month earlier. Her eldest daughter, Paige, confirmed her suspicions the last time she brought the grandkids by the house. Jaundice. The obstruction keeping her liver from properly doing its jobs was identified as a "racquetball-sized tumor" located on the top half of Janice's pancreas. Due to the tumor's size and location, surgery wasn't an option at this time without chemo and radiation treatments first. She kept the news to herself—not wanting to worry anyone. Martin hadn't noticed the jaundice, and not because he never stared deeply into her eyes, but rather because he did it so often. He hadn't noticed the gradual change. He only saw his wife.

She worried about Martin. What would become of him? She knew it was unfair of her to abandon him like this—to leave him with a herd of orphaned mules to take care of in his later years. Many of the mules would outlive him, she thought. Then, they would become the girls' problem to deal with. But who knows, maybe the drought will have let up by then.

Janice stood firm, and Martin caved. One more donkey wouldn't change things that much. They had to give the poor creatures a chance, a home, a place to be.

***

Robert Lee

Barbara leaned over in her chair, and the cat acted offended by the disturbance, hopping to the floor and tossing a nasty look over his shoulder as he sauntered from the room. Barbara lifted the shade to peek at her brittle yellow lawn. Thank goodness George wasn't alive to see this. The yard had been a great source of pride to him. Now even the prickly pear, the hardiest flora to be found in this arid country, shriveled in the miserable heat. Robert Lee was now well into stage three drought precautions. All households were asked to reduce their water usage by thirty percent. Barbara did her part, saving her bath water for several days at a time and reheating it for each use. Of course, any form of outdoor watering had been banned, though there were numerous reports of illegal late-night waterings in the news every day. Names and addresses were called out in hopes of shaming the culprits into cooperation.

She wondered if George would have been one of those names, his obsessiveness about lawn care overcoming his moral compass and sense of community. The funny thing was that he'd been dead for so long now, she wasn't even sure how he'd react to all this. After all, people change. And as George used to say, "Adapt or get left behind."

***

Levelland

Willie Stenson stood at the kitchen window of the old ranch style home where he'd been raised, sipping his decaf and watching as his father piddled around the yard. The horizon drew a straight line across the distance, and the red sun subtly inched its way down. Though Willie couldn't quite put his finger on it, there had been a distinct moment when his father *became* old, like that moment when the sun disappears into the earth. It was as if his father had aged so gradually that the actual change came suddenly—where old man strength just became old. He watched as his father struggled with the tailgate on his late '90s Dodge and wondered if he should go help him, then paused, and decided to wait until the old man got it on his own.

Once the gate was down, his father retrieved an orange and white Gott cooler, which was about the same age as Willie, if not older, from the bed of the truck and began to fish out a Miller Lite. Water dripped from the can, and the old man wiped it off with his shirt. Willie topped off his coffee, grabbed the brochures from the table, and went to join his father.

"Hey, Pop, can I grab your ear for a minute?"

"Don't see why not." Nolan Stenson attempted to hop onto the tailgate of his truck, but his knees weren't cooperating. "Here, boy, give me a hand, will ya?"

Willie wondered what his father did on evenings when he wasn't there to help him. Did he use a ladder? A stepstool? There's no way Willie's frail mother could help. She'd break under the strain.

"Watcha got there, Will?"

"It's what I wanted to talk to you about."

The old man scanned his son with suspicion. "Hmm." He hesitated, choosing his words carefully. "I guess if you live long enough this conversation is inevitable."

The Stenson family has always been known for their deliberate speaking style. They all do it, as if it were ingrained in their DNA. Of course, in Willie's case, it appeared to have skipped a generation, making him the fast-talking outcast at all the family functions. His cousin, Henry, dubbed him *The Salesmen*.

"What are you talking about, Pop?"

"I mean there comes a time in every man's life when his kids show up at the house with a handful of brochures talking about how it'll be better for all involved and about how great the food is and whatnot."

"Dad, you got me all wrong," Willie said, laughing at the miscommunication. He handed his father the brochures and hopped up on the tailgate next to him.

"Wanna beer?" Nolan asked.

"I got coffee."

"What are ya, a Baptist?"

"No, an alcoholic. You know that."

"And what's that say about me?" For some unknown reason, Nolan took his son's sobriety personally, like it meant he'd failed him as a father.

"I told you, I don't have your self-control. *A beer* is never just *a beer*."

Nolan nodded as he surveyed the pamphlet he'd been handed. "Sesame, huh? This again? I thought we were done with this."

"Hear me out. Cotton prices are pretty good right now, but—"

“Ain’t no *but* about it. Eighty-six cents a pound the last time I checked.”

“And yeah, that’s great. The problem is that without rain, our cotton is stressed. Our yields haven’t been good. You add in the costs of herbicides, insecticides, irrigation, and fertilizer and we’re barely making it.”

“I can’t argue with that.” The old man sipped his beer. “I gotta be honest with you, Will. I don’t even know what a *sesame* is, much less anything about farming'm.”

Willie knew this was an exaggeration, a technique his father had mastered during his forty-nine years of marriage—feigned ignorance. There was an orange and purple tint to the sky with streaks of blue peeking out as the sun looked to be only a few feet from touching the ground.

“What I do know is that it brings in less money and it’s a real bitch to harvest,” Nolan said.

“The revenues are less, but the crop itself is more reliable and uses a lot less water, like a quarter as much.”

“I told you about the mess I had when I tried to switch to milo. The damn mice about broke me.”

“The mice don’t like it,” Willie said.

“If the mice don’t like it, then who does?” The old man scoffed and took another swallow from his beer. A small dirt devil was picking up speed in the field before them, a tiny red twister.

“They put it on stuff like hamburger buns and muffins and high-end breads and the like. Don’t play dumb. You know exactly what it is. Plus, the Asians love it."

"Like China?"

"Like Asia. Like all of it."

The old man nodded. It had made a dent. Willie continued.

"You know what they say, 'Five billion Chinamen can't be wrong.'"

"Five billion? Jesus, is there that many of'm?"

"There's a lot for sure. Apparently, they use it for cooking oil, and they use that in everything."

"They're not a very big people. Do they eat much?"

"They eat enough and they got the numbers to make up for it." Willie directed his father's attention to one of the brochures that read *Sesaco* across the top. "Look, Pops, there's this company in Austin that's developed a shatter-resistant seed that can be machine harvested. We'll spend less money on chemicals and fertilizer, and we barely gotta water it. It's our best shot at surviving another dry year." For a second, the little tornado looked like it might come right at them, but instead it played tag with the earth and changed directions. The sun sank, baptized by the infinity of red dirt spread across the distance.

"I can remember when this field was cotton as far as the eye could see. An ocean of white gold. My father farmed this land long before you or the new house or me or any of it. It's always been cotton. Good years and bad." The old man kicked his feet in the air like a child on a swing. "I don't know if I have it in me—old dog, new tricks and all."

"Pop, it's not like you do the actual farming anymore. You've got me and a crew for that. We've got machines. The land needs a break. We've gotta try something different. And this is the answer."

"It's funny how slow the sun sinks for so long right up until that moment it finally hits the ground, and then it just disappears into nothin'. It's just there one second and gone the next."

"So, what do you think?"

Nolan drained his beer, crumpled the can, and tossed it over his shoulder into the bed of the truck. "About the sesame?" He cleared his throat. "I reckon five billion Chinamen can't *all* be wrong, can they?"

"You'll try it?"

"Beats the old folks' home."

"Or the poorhouse, for that matter."

"Yeah, I don't wanna live there neither." The old man scooted his butt off the tailgate and began to make his way back to the house. He teetered when he walked.

After a moment, Willie followed him in.

***

Robert Lee

Perhaps the biggest slap in the face to the water-starved residents of Robert Lee was that just twelve miles up the road lay the town of Bronte, which enjoyed a kind of water prosperity that mocked its parched neighbors to the west. Bronte's water wells were abundant and wealthy—overflowing. And the great miracle that everyone in Robert Lee hung their hats on was a million-dollar pipeline to Bronte—twelve miles of ten-inch pipe pumping 200,000 gallons daily. Provided they could get the money together and the permission, the project was expected to take about two months to complete. The news displayed a telephone number between segments where members of the community could call and find out how they could volunteer with the pipeline's construction or donate money to the cause. Barbara gave at the church.

"Our lawns will be green again," proclaimed a local politician that Barbara faintly recalled voting for. The woman's name ran across the bottom of the screen, but ever since they changed the shape of televisions things like this always seemed to get cut off on Barbara's old square set. Besides, even with her glasses, she would have struggled to see such small type. Still, the woman on TV looked familiar.

"Was she the one who came by the house? We had tea, didn't we?" Barbara reflected. "Kathy? Kate? Katie? Come on, Barb, think." She paused and thought long and hard. It was definitely a K-something. "Oh well, tea sounds nice. Maybe chamomile."

***

Bastrop

The wind was gusty atop the roof of the big two-story colonial that Jason Morales had sacrificed his Labor Day weekend to in order to finish the job early and pick up another one. He stood to give his knees and back a break and wiped his forehead with a tattered washcloth. A blast of hot air hit him square in the face and his balance faltered. It had to be blowing at thirty miles an hour or more. And that's when he saw it—the black cloud of smoke creeping in from the east, blanketing its path with a pool of grey shadows. Jason stared into it, trying to decipher whether it had made it to his place yet or not. Unsure, he pulled out his phone—*8 missed calls*. He dialed his wife.

"Where are you and the kids?"

"I've been trying to call you."

"Ringer was off. What the hell's going on, Teresa?"

"It's some kind of fire. We got evacuated. The sheriff came to the house and everything. Don't worry, I've got the boys. We're heading to my sister's."

"That serious?" He stopped. Horror struck him. "Please tell me you grabbed the box." There was silence. "Teresa?"

More silence.

"I told you the sheriff was there."

"Jesus, Teresa. Can you go back?" His voice desperate.

"I'm already in Austin, and I'm not turning back. Maybe if you'd pick up your phone once in a while."

"Everything we have is in there. Why didn't you grab it—throw it in a duffle bag and take it with you?" He clinched his fist and tried to keep his composure while his heart raced like a hamster on a wheel.

"First off, there's no way that lockbox would fit into a duffle bag. It's too big and boxy. It's heavy, too. Secondly, I'm not an idiot. Only a moron would risk grabbing your stupid box full of pot and drug money while getting escorted out by the goddamn sheriff."

Jason doubted that the sheriff had been hovering over her and the children as she packed their bags the way she tried to make it sound. He figured in truth, the lawman had asked her to vacate and then moved on to the neighbors up the road. Taking the box with her would have been totally feasible. She just didn't think about it.

He hung up the phone, climbed down from the roof, and sprinted to his truck. The radio described the fire as "volcanic, swallowing entire neighborhoods." The dry Texas summer had turned the pines into matchsticks and the gulf winds from Tropical Storm Lee acted like jet fuel spreading the flames across the landscape. There were reports of picket fences melting from the heat, and still Jason drove toward it. He thought about the day he'd purchased the lockbox. For seventeen dollars more, he could have bought the fireproof one.

When he got to the turnoff, he saw the flashing lights of the squad car parked at the convenience store and quickly turned his head away, acting as though he hadn't noticed it. If he got stopped, he'd plead ignorance. Maybe make up a story about an old relative who needed assistance.

He figured he still had some time if the cop was hanging out at the gas station. If there was a worse place to be during a fire, Jason couldn't think of it. The flames didn't look too far off, though. The cab of the truck was noticeably warmer. Jason's throat felt like it had been scraped by sandpaper as the thick fog choked his lungs and made it hard for him to see. He accelerated onto the gravel road that led to his family's small rented singlewide trailer, which sat on a piece of land they also did not own.

The box guarded what remained of a pound of fronted Afghan Kush. *Fronted* meaning *not yet paid for*. The box also held every dollar Jason had been able to save over the last two and a half years since his son, Michael, was first diagnosed as autistic—$10,286. He whipped the truck into the ruts that made up the driveway, threw it into park, and stripped the keys from the ignition. Sweat poured from him like it had that time in junior high when he gave his presentation on Sam Houston in front of the entire school. The eighth graders heckled him, and he forgot everything he was supposed to say.

With the same wildness of panic he'd felt on that day, he now fumbled with the keys unlocking the trailer door. It was getting harder to breathe. He pulled his shirt over his face, but the thin cotton did little to protect him from the smoke. His washcloth was still in the truck. Inside the trailer, he flicked on the light and took one last look around the room. Woozy in the sweltering heat, he made his way to the bedroom. He pulled the box from the closet, but decided he couldn't haul it out exposed like that—if someone saw him carrying it, they'd immediately assume its contents were illegal in nature. He needed to conceal it somehow. He ran to the small laundry area located by the back door of the trailer, grabbed a basket that contained a set of pee-stained Batman sheets and matching pajamas, and went back to the bedroom to retrieve his family's lifesavings. The heat was becoming unbearable. There was a blurriness to the inside of the trailer—the way asphalt looks in the summer. He shoved the lockbox into the laundry basket, burying it in the urine-soaked Batman merchandise. He then went to the dresser and grabbed a couple of bandanas to tie across his face, figuring it was better than nothing. He was on the run now. There wasn't much time.

A wave of relief hit as his tires left the gravel behind and got on the main road. The cop at the gas station was gone. The black sky crept upon him, and his foot became heavy, driving the gas pedal into the floorboard. He didn't breathe again until he hit traffic on 71. Jason reached into his back pocket for his phone so he could call Teresa and let her know he was okay. The phone wouldn't come on—lifeless. He looked at it. The four corners were melted inward.

"Should've bought the insurance," he said to himself as he tossed the phone across the cab of the truck and drove on.

***

Robert Lee

Barbara pulled herself up and out of her chair. Her slippers shuffled across the floor and into the kitchen. The cat rubbed up against her legs, insisting on being fed. Barbara retrieved the leftover tuna from the fridge and bent to scoop it into Shelby's bowl. She washed her hands and filled the teapot with just enough water for one cup and set it on the stove. When she shut off the faucet, two quick drops plummeted into the sink basin. Then, a third. Then, nothing.

THE SOLICITATION OF TOM W

Between job interviews at the few remaining ad agencies willing to return his calls, Tom W squeezed in a two o'clock meeting at St. Andrew's on 42nd. It wasn't one of his usual spots, but he needed the pick-me-up to compensate for a morning filled with disappointment.

After introducing himself from the podium at the front of the room, he told his fellow alcoholics how he'd lost his job. A few people snickered, others cringed. He then told the story about how he backed over the family's beloved and aging Golden Retriever, Milo, and how his two beautiful daughters, now seven and ten, still found this act unforgivable. He spoke of how his wife gave him "plenty of chances" and how he blew them all. And when he was done speaking, the room full of strangers thanked him for his honesty and courage as he took his seat between the old guy with the twitch and the young woman with the burn scars. He greeted both with a smile. The old man gave a sort of head nod, which may have been involuntary, and the young woman turned her head away and fixed her eyes on a poster of a weary marathon runner nearing the finish line. The caption on the poster read: *Almost There!*

In true A.A. form, the coffee was stale and the people damaged. Tom W felt right at home in his metal folding chair, though it creaked under his weight. Meanwhile, a nervous woman in a blue floral print muumuu read the Tenth Step from the

Big Book, and Tom W tried to pay attention. He hated the Tenth. His life was an utter cesspool, which made his Daily Inventories a torturous procedure. But like all secret societies, A.A. was full of seemingly ridiculous rituals and their unquestioned repetition, and Tom W, in his desperation, tried his best to abide and follow the program.

***

In the subway, after his last interview of the day, two trains passed before him in a clash of light and sound that rattled every cheap filling in his head. He shuddered at the thought of another month on unemployment and then reminded himself to be thankful for the few blessings he had left. He felt broken—shattered, even. He wanted a drink and he wanted it bad. He began to sweat. Clearing his throat, he choked momentarily. If only he could be that lucky—to die suddenly—anonymously. He scanned the platform, found a place to sit, and waited for the next train.

He was short and stout, almost perfectly round—middle-aged and violently bald. His hairline had long since receded, now taking up residency in thick patches along his back and shoulders. This retreat, along with everything else that made him feel inferior, had given him a crippling fear of his own repulsive nudity. The idea of dating seemed so far out of his reach that he wondered how he had ever gotten Vera to fall in love with him in the first place. Though her figure was no longer what it once was, he knew she'd have no shortage of suitors, all better looking and more successful than he was. The best he could say for himself was that he was now six months, two weeks, and three days sober. He found pride in this fact and often thought that he should wear one of those signs around his neck that read: *199 Days Without an Accident*. One more day would make an even 200—a milestone. And that was the point: it was all about One Day At A Time.

But weren't those days supposed to get easier? Instead, every day he felt like he was dragging an anchor up a steep hill through a hailstorm of fear and failure. The anchor kept getting heavier and the hail more piercing. *Quit focusing on the negative,* he told himself. *So what if your wife left you and your ungrateful kids despise you and nobody in this lousy town will hire your sorry ass to save your worthless godforsaken life? At least you're sober. At least you're making an effort. Get through today. Tomorrow is 200. Almost There.*

As he waited for his train, he tapped out a rhythm on the armrest of the bench. This was a nervous habit he'd developed as a child. The tune was always the same, the theme from the old *Dick Van Dyke Show*. It used to drive Vera crazy. As he tapped out the finale, he caught sight of a discarded classifieds section with a personal ad circled in thick red ink: *Got Herpes? Me, too! Sometimes love hurts.* He had to laugh. He thanked God for His sense of humor. Surrendering one's self to a Higher Power was an important part of the program, even for non-believers, and Tom W was willing to try anything. He liked to think of his life as God's favorite sitcom, a comedy based around a bumbling protagonist who never won but always entertained.

The station rumbled as his train pulled up and eased to a stop. He gathered his leather-bound portfolio folder and boarded, loathing public transportation almost as much as job interviews. The irony: an advertising executive who could no longer sell himself. Twenty years in the business, a bookshelf full of awards, and the genius behind some of the best-loved ads around had all been torn down by a moment of inappropriate behavior caught on some asshole's camera phone at a Christmas party.

It had happened sometime after polishing off the second bottle of scotch, a twelve-year-old single malt if memory served, though the rest of the details remained blurry. Of course, thanks to the Internet, he had put together the majority of the missing pieces. It went like this: Tom W, 2012 Northeastern Regional Advertising Man of the Year, for some unknown reason decided to "motorboat" the seventy-something-year-old wife of the chief CEO of the prestigious Bullock and Sellers Agency. The pictures went viral via the advertising community and were linked to the grossly popular YouTube video: *Fat Man Motorboats Grandma!*

With over a million hits in the first week, Tom W became the wrong kind of famous.

Still, if you asked Vera or his daughters, killing Milo was worse.

***

On the train, he watched a young woman making her way through the car. Mid-to-late twenties, long dirty-blonde hair, a little curvy for his tastes but cute and casual. She wore a clingy orange and blue sundress and she carried a clipboard as she engaged various passengers in conversations, occasionally getting signatures. What was she selling? He tried not to judge her solicitous behavior as she made her way toward him. Their eyes met. She approached.

"Sir, would you like to do your part to save the planet?" Her tone was upbeat, her smile pleasant and distracting.

"Uh, excuse me?" He was buying time, trying to think of something clever.

"Would you like to do your part to save the planet?" Again, she smiled.

"Um, no, not enough to join Greenpeace or anything. I'll be lucky if I can save myself at this rate."

She laughed and playfully patted him on the chest. He flexed involuntarily—as if he had a shot with this girl. She continued her spiel, and he nodded with envy for her passion.

"Do you ride the train to lighten your carbon footprint?"

"Uh, no. After my third DWI, the state decided to *lighten* my carbon footprint for me." Something about her put him at ease. He felt a swagger that had been absent since his last drink.

"Oh, I'm sorry." Her eyes glazed over with a touch of pity, or was it concern?

"Yup, before that I drove a Hummer that ran on rain forests and puppies."

It took her a second, but again she laughed and patted. "Very funny. You're mocking me, aren't you?"

"No." He paused. "Well, maybe a little." He did his best to smile. Though he knew she was only flirting with him to make the sale, his confidence grew.

"Come on, wouldn't you like to save the polar bears?" she asked. "I mean, their habitats are, like, melting and they're facing extinction in our lifetimes." She dug through her purse to retrieve a dog-eared photo of a pathetic-looking polar bear, more brown than white, as if it were spoiling in the sun like a piece of fruit. It reminded him of the dog he'd killed—poor Milo. The dog that hadn't died right away. The dog that whined all the way to the twenty-four-hour vet clinic before finally being put down. Those sad eyes going blank in an instant.

"My God, he looks like I feel," Tom W said, and gave the girl a wink which he immediately regretted.

She looked at him as if he were a curiosity.

"Look, I wish I could help," he said. "I really do, but I've actually got a pretty serious vendetta against polar bears. In fact, they're my sworn enemies."

"You're kidding, right?"

He made his face look stern.

"How can you hate polar bears?" she asked.

He felt like she had to know he was messing with her again, but she took the bait.

"One killed my cat in a knife fight, and I've never gotten over it."

She laughed, again. She ran her hand down his left arm, lingering at the wrist for a few seconds before letting go. He trembled.

"You're pretty funny, aren't you?" she said.

"I have my moments."

"I bet you do—hey, I don't normally do this, but I kind of have a weird thing for guys like you."

"Do you mean *distinguished and charming* or *bald and rotund*?" His smile, he felt, was boyish and playful. She was definitely flirting. He didn't understand why.

"Can it be a little of both?" she asked.

"Wow, that is weird," he said.

He thought about his own daughters, much too young for dating now, but it was only matter of time before they'd be flirting with old, fat men on trains. A horrifying thought. Surely his girls would have better taste. Then again, didn't women always go for men like their fathers? Perhaps it was good that his daughters hated him—for their sake.

"I bet you have a hairy back, don't you? In the gay community, guys like you are called *Bears*," she said.

"And what about in the straight community?"

"I don't know. Can't I just call you cute?"

"So, you've really got a thing for bears, polar or otherwise?"

"Yeah, I guess I do." Her blues eyes lit up. "My name is Amber." She held her hand out in that dainty way of girls who grew up believing they were princesses, and Tom W took it like a gentleman and kissed it lightly. Her skin smelled like mangos.

"Of course it is. I knew you were an *Amber* the second I laid eyes on you," he said. "People call me Tom."

"Nice to meet you, Tom," she said as she did a kind of bow and curtsy thing with the hem of her dress. "Can I ask you something?"

"Anything."

"Well, this might sound kind of crazy. I don't know you or what your plans are for this evening and all, but would you like to grab a drink with me?" Her eyes drew him in. Everything else drifted away. The train, the other passengers, the meetings, the ex-wife, the kids, the dog, and even the failed interviews all got lost in the moment.

Tom W started to speak but hesitated. His sobriety pulled him back. The whining cries of the dying dog echoed through the hallways of his mind. Vera and his daughters' faces; cruel and full of hate, just like the day he moved out, flashed before his eyes. He looked at the girl in front of him, and somehow, she appeared different. Was it innocence or something else? Whatever it was, he knew he couldn't do what he wanted to do. He gathered himself.

"Sweetheart," he said, his voice shaky. "You have no idea how much I'd like to have a drink with you, but unfortunately I have to pass." He took a deep breath before continuing. "Maybe some other time."

Even Tom W was shocked by his words. She didn't seem like a girl who got turned down often, certainly not by guys like him. In fact, he was probably her first. She shrank under his rejection, and his heart mourned the loss, but it was a matter of self-preservation. She thanked him for his time and disappeared into the crowd with her clipboard and convictions, the tight-fitting orange and blue sundress etched into his brain. He envied her and despised himself.

***

That night at his ten o'clock meeting, he introduced himself as "Tom W" once again and told his story. He spoke of the wife, the kids, the dog, the career, the girl on the train, and of polar bears. Tears ran down his cheeks, and his nose began to run as he made his way back to his seat. They thanked him for sharing. They always thanked you.

THE DUKE OF CORDILLERA

Once a strong and intelligent woman, Ann Greenwood found she no longer possessed the wit of her youth. Her memory had begun fading faster than her husband's hearing—most likely due to the pugilistic dementia she'd suffered during a freak accident at a family funeral. Her conversation with Cousin Gary that morning had been an in-depth one. Everyone could agree on that. In fact, the normally surefooted Ann had become so distracted by whatever Gary had to say that she completely missed the six-inch change in elevation from curb to street and landed face first onto the concrete. For weeks after, Ann refused to leave the house for fear that people might think her husband, Bill, was to blame for the bruises painted across her face. As for the subject of that conversation with Cousin Gary, it remained a family mystery. Ann couldn't for the life of her remember, and Cousin Gary's funeral came shortly after.

The Greenwoods did not attend.

***

Ann felt sharpest in the mornings. As the days dragged on, she became tired and things slipped through the cracks. It was exhausting. And she knew everyone was talking about it. Her memory loss sat like a giant elephant squeezed into a tiny room. She pictured it, alongside the relatives at a family gathering, stuffing its trunk with fried okra and coleslaw. Oh, how they loved to talk. She'd heard them.

"She asks me what we're having for dinner a hundred times a night. And I say, 'Damn it, Annie, I just told you,'" Bill told Janet's husband, Stan, while piling brisket onto a paper plate. His voice carried.

"What are you gonna do?"

"I don't know, but it's getting to the point where I'm afraid to leave her at the house by herself."

"You're kidding. I didn't realize it had gotten that bad."

Ann hadn't either. She couldn't believe her ears—sold out by her own husband. Betrayed. He knew she was self-conscious about this. Embarrassed by it all, she began to develop coping skills. She created a system of Post-it notes and detailed schedules and routines to help keep her on track. Daily dinner menus were stuck to the glass of the microwave door in case she forgot. She quit thinking for herself all together, adopting her husband's opinions and nodding emphatically to the points he made. She observed everyone closely and spoke less and less. If she did speak, it was always in vague generalities. She used ambiguous language and catch phrases she'd stolen from *Fox News*.

"Well, I just think he's an Obamanation. And besides, we still haven't seen his birth certificate," she would contribute when she felt it suitable. Otherwise, she'd nod and smile and look to her husband for the appropriate response or reaction.

For a while, this seemed to work. Ann could tell Bill believed, or at least wanted to believe, that his wife's condition might be improving because he stopped mentioning it to the doctor. Ann, of course, knew it wasn't true, but she'd also never been one for doctors or medication.

Perhaps the worst part of all of this was the thought of being left alone with her only grandchild. When Sara first married Colin, Ann caught a severe case of the *grandmother fever*. And now that she finally had one of her very own, she feared she might break it. After all, she told herself, babies are fragile.

***

Bill Greenwood, Ann's husband of more than forty years, was a man who'd been called many things in his life, both to his face and behind his back, but never "soft." Ann even struggled at times to break through the hard shell that encased her husband's gruff heart. Still, she knew he loved her. And it didn't matter that he was difficult, short-tempered, stubborn, and way too hard on the kids—he was a good provider and there comes a point in every woman's life where that becomes enough.

When the kids were little, Bill's two favorite sayings around the Greenwood house were: "I'll tell you what *The Golden Rule* is. It's simple. The man with the gold rules," and "Nobody likes a whiner." Raised on the edge of The Depression and fueled by the nationalism of WWII, Bill's philosophy on life raged pure American bootstrapping—a republican to the end, a Marine Corps Officer in Korea, and an Okie from Muskogee who had never taken a single trip on LSD as he so proudly reminded Ann every time that particular song came on the radio. His life and work were one. His nights were not spent at PTA meetings or ballgames or dance recitals. He lived in the office. Ann imagined him sitting at his desk contemplating a wounded economy and nursing a bottle of scotch. And when he came home, work came with him.

Even in retirement he worked every problem into the ground until he was confident he'd found the right answer. If Ann needed a new dishwasher, Bill did the research. And when the dishwasher was purchased, delivered, installed, and officially up and running, Bill moved on to the next problem. Scotch remained a major part of Bill's process. His internal bar clock, he told her, officially opened at 5 p.m., though sometimes closer to 4:30, or even 4. In his retirement, Bill allowed himself the luxury of opening the bar much earlier. Ann noticed but never said anything. In fact, she usually had whatever he was having.

The Greenwood daily ritual became a beer or three at lunch, scotch and waters while throwing peanuts and stale Goldfish to the dogs in the mid-to-late afternoon, and red wine during dinner before switching to brandy in the evenings. Brandy replaced cognac as Bill and Ann's dessert beverage of choice because they were disappointed in the French—untrustworthy cowards that they were.

Every night, Ann, slight as she was, held her own. And, oddly enough, she tended to hold her liquor much better than her husband. When bedtime arrived, Ann would shift into designated driver mode, guiding Bill from the couch to the bedroom as he pinballed down the long hall of their retirement dream home. Cordillera Ranch was located in the middle of nowhere as far as Ann was concerned, a gated rural community about forty-five miles northwest of San Antonio. The Greenwood's home sat nestled atop the closest thing to a mountain the Texas Hill Country had to offer. And if Ann didn't take care of Bill, then who would? Too many nights, he fell and hurt himself—his skin paper thin. And when the drink became too much and Bill got sick, Ann was there to help him to the bathroom and quietly clean up his mess as he drunkenly professed his love for her and the kids.

"I just love you sooo much, dear," he'd say. "I don't know what I did to d-d-deserve you. I just can't artic-artic-cu-late how much, how-how much, you and the kids mean to me. So much, dear."

"I know, dear," Ann would say.

On the rare mornings when Bill recalled the events from the night before, he often blamed the dogs for his early start.

"Duke and Lizzie don't understand daylight savings time. They think it's time for snacks, and you know how Duke gets."

It was true. The dog could be demanding.

***

Duke increasingly became a problem within the Greenwood family dynamic. A picture-perfect example of a German Shorthaired Pointer in the prime of his life, Ann could tell the dog saw himself as the alpha of the house. In true Shakespearean form, she thought, he'd used his friendship with the king to usurp the power of the throne and pretty much do as he pleased. Ann had always enjoyed Shakespeare in school and began to call the dog *The Duke of Cordillera*. Bill, however, didn't care for the nickname, and so it never stuck.

The other dog, Lizzie, was nothing more than a lackey. A Home Depot parking lot rescue, she was indebted to Duke for showing her the boundaries of the invisible fence and allowing her to stay on the property. Ann dubbed the heeler mix "Licky Lizzie" for the way she timidly shied away whenever confronted by new humans, only to sneak her way back and lick the hand of the strangers who passed her screening process. She became Ann's dog because Bill's stern voice and manner frightened her. Duke and Bill, however, were partners.

The solution to another problem thoroughly worked out by her husband, Bill hand-picked and paid for the pointer in order to replace Hawk, his aging Brittany Spaniel, who was getting too old to hunt at the time. Thirty-five hundred was more than Bill had ever spent on a dog, but Duke was no ordinary dog. His physique, markings, and pedigree were outstanding—the perfect genetically engineered quail dog. The Brittany had been too fragile, his feet too soft, his coat too long and too brown. He often got lost in the brush and his hair always got twisted and matted with sticker burrs. And perhaps worst of all, Hawk was prone to retreating beneath the truck whenever challenged by larger males—a lover, not a fighter. Ann knew this embarrassed her husband to no end.

The two dogs never got along, Duke and Hawk. By eight months, Duke towered over the Brittany and began to bully him. There was a sense that Duke welcomed his elder's death in much the same way that a farmer welcomes the first rain. He moved up in the order of command and took his place next to the king. Lizzie joined the family about a year later.

By the time Grandson Tommy came along, Duke was four and a half and well-established in the household. After his opportunities to hunt diminished, due to Bill and Ann's health problems, the dog took over security detail by patrolling the perimeter throughout the day and unleashing his most vicious front upon all who entered the Greenwood home. When Daniel, Ann's only boy, retired from the Marine Corp and moved to the outskirts of San Antonio, just thirty minutes from his parents, Duke lost his mind. The dog tried on several occasions to nip the prodigal son, but the prodigal son moved too quickly. Eventually, Daniel nipped back and bloodied the dog's nose with a right cross. The issue was settled. Daniel had earned the dog's respect. Ann witnessed the event but chose not to tell her husband. It didn't seem necessary.

Others weren't as lucky as Daniel and were bullied by the stoic pointer. In particular, the dog disliked Colin, Sara's off-the-boat Irish bartender husband, because Bill disliked Colin. Every time the couple came to visit from Austin, something unpleasant would happen.

"Everybody knows that dogs are the best judges of character," Bill would say.

"Look at how cautious Lizzie is around Colin."

"Dad, that's not fair. She's afraid of everyone," Sara would say.

When little Tommy was about nine months old, the dog established his authority over the child. No one knew exactly what had happened that day because no one actually saw it transpire, but the child was visibly traumatized.

"What do you expect?" Bill said. "He scoots around here screaming and yelling with those damn blaring toy trucks and their sirens. Duke answered the noise complaint. I don't even know why you and Colin bother coming out here. You spend all your time messing with the baby when you do."

"He's nine months, Dad. We have to keep an eye on him all the time. That's part of the job. See what happens when we turn our backs for even a second?"

"I just think Colin monopolizes the boy."

"It's called parenting. You and mom never make an effort to connect with Tommy. That's not Colin's fault. Besides, that's not the point. Your *fucking* dog attacked my child!"

"Don't be hysterical. That's your version of it. Duke says he was following protocol," Bill said, rubbing the dog's big brown ears in front of his daughter.

Sara's words hurt her mother. Ann wanted to play with Tommy but didn't know how. But her daughter was right about Bill. He had never shown much interest in the kids. He was the breadwinner and disciplinarian. That pretty much summed up the extent of his parental contribution. As a grandfather, he wasn't much better.

"You need to stop mothering the boy. You don't want him to grow up to be a pussy, do you?"

Ann cringed and left the room. Sara packed up her family, crying child and all, and headed back to Austin.

In the months that followed, the child's fear of dogs only confirmed Bill's suspicion of his daughter's "mothering."

"We're a dog family," he explained to Ann.

To Bill, a grandson that cries and screams for his mommy every time a dog comes within ten feet of him was unacceptable. It was the equivalent of hiding under the truck. Ann didn't know what to say.

***

Daniel's return to the flock a few years later provided the one hope that the child might be rescued from his canine phobia. Daniel seldom went anywhere without his best friend and sidekick; a slightly overweight redheaded yellow lab mix with the disposition of a kindly old nanny from a children's story. Ginger's public exposure around the base had allowed her the opportunity to master the art of being non-threatening. She tagged along on daily errands and slept peacefully at the foot of

Daniel's bed. He referred to her as his "old ball and chain." Ann thought this was funny, though she did wish her son would settle down and meet a nice girl.

It didn't take long for Ginger's laid-back demeanor to win over the frightened child. Ann watched. The dog was so gentle and sweet, moving slow and deliberate. Ann wished it could be that easy for her. Ginger's maternal nature lured the boy in as he cautiously faced his fear. Over time, Tommy began to play with the dog, even asking to sleep with her in his bed whenever Daniel's visits overlapped with theirs. This made Ann happy. She tried to explain to Tommy that Lickie Lizzy was more afraid of him than he was of her, and he seemed to understand.

Duke, however, was still a wildcard and not to be trusted. Ann couldn't really fault the child for that.

***

On the eve before Tommy's second Christmas, as Colin and Daniel pieced together a train set in the living room and Tommy slept, most likely with visions of sugarplums in his head, Ann made her way down the long hall to the rear of the house to let the dogs in. It was a cold night and Duke, with his thin coat, usually bedded down in his doghouse for warmth. When Ann reached her hand inside the small lean-to, the dog jumped and snapped three times viciously. She yanked her arm back and almost fell over backward. Her skin was thin from age and alcohol, and the blood poured from her veins. She didn't scream. She didn't cry. She did not make a sound. Ann didn't want to bother anyone. She just let the dogs back into the house and set about silently rinsing the wound in the utility room sink.

When Daniel found her twenty minutes later, the scene looked like a set from a cheap horror film—blood on the walls, the floors, the countertops—blood everywhere.

The wound became infected, and Ann's tiny little forearm swelled up to near Popeye proportions and landed her a two-week's stay in the Methodist hospital in San Antonio. She missed Christmas and New Years that year, and she pleaded with the staff on a daily basis to allow her to return home to her Post-it notes, routines, and carefully planned schedules. It scared her when she woke in the night and couldn't find Bill, or worse, had no clue where she was. She felt helpless, restrained by IV tubes and hospital corners—trapped. Despite all of this, Ann took the blame for what happened that night.

"I shouldn't have startled him like that," she insisted to anyone who asked.

The details of the second attack on Ann remained less clear, but the end result was the same—infection, swelling, and a two-week's stay at Methodist. Again, she took the blame.

"It happened fast," she told the doctor. "I must've given him a scare."

In truth, like the conversation with Cousin Gary, the events of the attack were lost. She simply couldn't remember what happened that night, and so Bill created his own version.

"It's her condition. She has these spells where she's just not herself. Hell, I don't even recognize her sometimes, and we've been married forty-six years. Duke probably thought he was reacting to a stranger—an intruder."

***

Over the next two years, the incidents increased in frequency, and it was never the dog's fault. The Cub Scout selling popcorn door-to-door for a fundraiser came next. The doorbell spun the dogs into a frenzy, and they pushed past Ann as she opened the door. The nine-year-old was greeted with a bite to the crotch.

"Dad, he bit a kid in the dick. Something is not right with that dog," Daniel told his father when he and sister made their first attempt at an intervention.

Ann sat silent throughout the proceedings.

"We don't know for sure it was Duke. Both dogs pushed past your mother and she didn't see what happened until it was too late."

"That's ridiculous," said Sara. "You have two dogs. One with a history of biting the *actual* hand that feeds it and the other who is terrified of strangers. We all know which dog did this."

"Technically, the boy was trespassing. The sheriff confirmed it. There's no soliciting in Cordillera. It's in the bylaws. If you ask me, it's the parents' fault. Who sends their kid out to hustle for handouts anyway?"

"You did. Don't you remember all the cookies I sold as a Girl Scout or the candy bars

Daniel hawked for baseball uniforms? Oh, wait, I forgot. You were never around when we were little. You were at the office."

"That's right. And when I was in scouts, we *worked* to raise money. That's the problem with your generation. Everybody wants a handout."

"You're impossible." Sara caught herself and took a deep breath before continuing. "You have to do something about that dog, or else I'm not bringing my son around here anymore."

Ann looked at her husband, her eyes starting to water. She wanted to speak up but couldn't find the words. No one would listen anyway.

"Stop being over-dramatic, Sara. It doesn't become you," Bill said, as he poured himself another drink.

"Dad, how can you not see the problem here?" Daniel said. "The dog has tried to bite me, Colin, and even Tommy. It put Mom in the hospital twice and now it's tried to re-circumcise a child."

"We don't know what happened with Tommy. Duke's just working security, running the perimeter, and trying to keep out the riffraff. Daniel, you of all people should be able to understand that."

"A Cub Scout is riffraff?" Sara cried from across the table. "Mom? Daniel? Your grandson? My husband? *Seriously?*"

"The jury is still out on Colin." Bill smiled.

Sara was not amused. Nor was Daniel.

"Dad, the dog is a problem. I think he thinks he's in charge. He doesn't respect your authority. In his mind, he's the pack leader. If you don't reestablish yourself as the alpha male, there's no telling what else he'll do."

Ann smiled. Daniel was saying what she wished she could. He was so calm, so rational. She was proud of the man he'd become.

"If you ask me, this shit's being blown out of proportion. The kid's britches took most of the damage. Duke barely broke the skin."

"The kid's probably going to be traumatized for the rest of his life," Daniel said. "I mean, luckily Tommy was young enough that he's starting to get over it, but that Cub Scout will always remember what Duke did to him."

"Barely broke the skin," Bill repeated.

Ann got up from the table and went to bed. The sun was still up.

***

Four months later, Bill was finally worn down into action when his veterinarian of eight years joined his offspring's cause. This time the vet's new assistant was to blame, improperly securing the dog during its annual shots. The vet had suffered worse bites in his long career and made little of the event. He did; however, due to the dog's history, suggest a canine psychologist.

Though it took a while to wrap his head around the concept of animal psychology, Bill gave the woman a call. She had a degree from Texas A&M.

"At least it'll get the kids off my back," he told Ann.

She nodded.

The diagnosis of the dog surprised no one. Frustrated by not being able to fulfill his duties as a retriever, Duke had taken over security, just as Bill had said. The psychologist also suggested that Daniel might be on to something with his power struggle theory, but Bill dismissed this. The woman suggested placing *Beware of Dog* signs at the entrance of the property and by the front door. She then prescribed what she referred to as "muzzle therapy," which would require Bill to wrestle an eighty-five-dollar Hannibal Lecter mask over the dog's snout three times a day for fifteen minutes a session. During these sessions, Bill was to periodically slide special treats into the gaps of the mask, making it a more pleasurable experience for the dog. Ann kept her distance as Bill administered this treatment. She could tell that Duke loved the treats but hated the mask.

Bill put the signs up himself. The children saw this all as a step in the right direction and let up on their father about the dog. Unfortunately, muzzle therapy was inconsistent at best and lasted less than a month before the dog convinced his owner to continue the treats without the humiliation of the mask. Still, Sara and Tommy began to visit again on the condition that Duke be kept outside whenever Tommy was inside and vice versa. This was easier said than done since Ann often forgot this rule and slipped back into her routine of *dog wants in—let dog in—dog wants out—let dog out*. Ann hated it every time she made this mistake with Duke and wished she could stick a Post-it note to the inside of her head that said *DUKE STAYS OUT*.

Several times a day, Sara could be heard saying, "Is Duke in the house? Who let Duke in?" She'd then rush to protect her child and insist that the dog be put back out. At night, after the toddler had been put to bed, Duke reclaimed his usual place in the home, only to be banished to the yard again in the morning. Meanwhile, Ginger and Lizzie were allowed full reign of the house. Tommy was comfortable with them, and everyone agreed that a reasonable solution had been found.

What Sara and Daniel didn't know was that there had been another incident, and Ann was sworn to secrecy. She repeated Bill's words to herself until she felt they were posted to her brain. She didn't want to slip up again and upset everyone.

***

The incident had happened on a Sunday. The satellite had gone out right before the Cowboys' first pre-season game of the year, and all hell broke loose in the Greenwood household. Bill wasn't a man who accepted "no" as an answer. He didn't care what day it was—he wanted it fixed. Ann felt sorry for the person on the other end of the phone as she listened to her husband's voice escalate.

The man who arrived an hour later was a subcontracted repairman sent out by the satellite company on his day off. He arrived early in the second quarter. Bill and Ann were in the front yard pulling weeds and listening to the game on a small black transistor radio they'd had since the seventies.

Seeing the dogs and the sign, the man paused his approach and asked, “Do your dogs bite?”

“The pointer does,” Bill replied as he began to get to his feet.

The man ignored this warning and continued forward. It happened in a flash. When it was over, the bites were minor, as the man had defended himself by landing his heavy steel-toed boot into the dog’s ribcage. The sheriff was called and again he deemed the matter out of his jurisdiction since the event occurred on the Greenwood’s property and the property was clearly marked with warning signs. If the man wished to make it a civil issue, that was up to him. And he did.

“That bastard is suing us,” Bill told his wife after picking up the mail one evening a few weeks later.

“Which bastard, dear?”

“The repairman—greedy piece of shit. I warned him, Annie. I told him. He’s looking for a score—a handout. You saw his hand—it was nothing. I would’ve poured rubbing alcohol on it and gone about my day if it had happened to me.”

“It’s Obama’s fault. He’s trying to turn us all into socialists,” Ann replied.

“Focus, dear. We *cannot* tell the kids about this. We’ll let the insurance company take care of it.”

“That’s probably best,” she said, now thinking that her husband was referring to a traffic ticket he’d recently received for rolling through a stop sign in town. "The insurance company will take care of everything," she repeated.

***

Tommy's fourth birthday came a little over a month later. The event was Batman-themed and held at the grandparents' house because they had the room. Ann had been surprised when she found Daniel showing her grandson the campy Adam West show from the '70s a few months earlier. She asked if it wasn't too much for a child his age, and Daniel assured her it wasn't. Tommy became obsessed with the show and demanded a Batman birthday party. Daniel went all out for his nephew. He dressed in a suit and played the part of Alfred, the butler. He even went to the trouble of creating a Batcave out of the long hallway and one of the guest bedrooms.

Seven mini-caped crusaders ran screaming all over the property as they fought the invisible criminal element that plagued the streets of Gotham City. Tommy was the undisputed leader of this ragtag Justice League thanks to a high-end and very muscular Batman costume he'd received from one of his Irish aunts.

Na, na, na, na, na, na, na, na, na, na, na, na, Batman!

Duke had been kenneled for the day at the Happy Paw Doggie Spa a few miles up the main road. His spa day included three twenty-minute stints in the common area, a six-by-six cell, and meals hand-delivered to his cage twice daily. Bill did his best to end the party early and clear the children from the premises so he could bail his buddy out before the kennel closed at 6 p.m. and he had to pay for a second day. They cut it close, but he and Ann made it just in time.

Ecstatic to be sprung from the joint, the dog eagerly waited for the birthday boy to be put to bed so that he could rejoin the family and the other dogs inside. Several times Ann saw him standing by the door and tried to let him in, but someone always stopped her. Wired from birthday sugar and the brand new Batman costume, Tommy was nowhere near bedtime. He was fighting it all the way, and Sara told her mother that she might "just let him wear himself out."

***

Bill was somewhere in the back of the house, Colin and Daniel were assembling toys in the living room, and Sara was elbow deep in dishes when Ann saw the dog waiting by the door and let him in. She then wandered into the kitchen to help her daughter with the cleanup so that they could all go to bed. It had been a long day and she was drained. She shuffled her feet across the tile floor as she collected more dishes from the table.

In an instant, the little boy's high-pitched screams echoed through the house. Bill apparently heard nothing. Ann became confused. Everyone else sprinted in the direction of the commotion. Ann followed.

The dog had the tiny superhero by the head, growly and violently clamping down. Daniel pried the dog's jaws loose, but Duke slipped free and went for Tommy's leg. The child's screams tore through

Ann as she watched. Still, Bill heard nothing. Ann stood frozen at the end of the hall not knowing what to do. With Colin and Sara's help, Daniel again pried the dog from the child and hauled him aggressively out of the house.

"I'm sorry," Ann said. "I'm really sorry."

"Jesus Christ, Mom, it's not your fault," Sara said, red-faced and pushing past her with the whimpering child in her arms.

***

It took forty minutes to drive to the hospital in San Antonio. Daniel drove his father's Buick, Colin cursed beneath his breath, and Sara did her best to keep her composure. Bill and Ann stayed behind and got the story secondhand from their son. Pictures were taken, reports filed, preventative shots administered. Seven staples were used to repair the child's head and a few in the lower back. Seventeen stitches laced up the gashes that wrapped their way around his leg, and medical glue was used for several other rips.

When it was all over and the hospital released the boy, Daniel drove his sister's family back to his house in town before returning his father's car. Drunk at the kitchen table, Bill stroked the dog's head with a tenderness he'd never shown his children or grandchild, Ann thought. And then she wondered about the clarity of that thought. Was it real? Was it hers? Her husband looked up when Daniel entered. The dogs barked.

"How bad is it?"

"Pretty bad. A shitload of staples and stitches and shit, but Tommy's taking it like a champ. Of course, he never wants to come back here again."

Bill nodded as he stared at the dog's head in his lap. "And Duke?"

Ann could see that her husband was hurting. She'd never seen him like this before—helpless with a problem he couldn't solve. At least, Ann couldn't recall ever seeing him like this before.

"I would expect a visit from the Animal Control people tomorrow if I were you."

Bill nodded a few times. "Can I get you a drink?"

"Please."

He got up to make his son a drink, and the dog followed. Lizzie snored from her spot under the table by Ann's feet. Something serious was going on. That much Ann knew.

***

The next morning, Bill and Daniel placed several phone calls and Ann helped her husband by typing out an email for his contacts list vaguely describing the dog's situation and need for a new a home. To Ann's surprise, tears ran down Bill's cheeks as she read it aloud for his approval.

Dear Friends,

I have always believed that there is no such thing as a bad dog, only bad owners. I regret to admit that Ann and I are bad owners. In our old age, we have failed our eight-year-old German

Shorthaired Pointer. Due to health problems, I have been unable to hunt Duke as much as he deserves and this has caused some serious behavioral problems in the dog. He needs an active home with a younger master than myself and should be kept away from children.

Please contact me immediately if you or anyone you know has a possible home for this fine bird dog.

Sincerely,
William S. Greenwood

By the time Animal Control arrived to quarantine the dog, Daniel was back at the house, and Bill had already received a possible lead—a friend of a friend looking for a dog to tight-kennel and take on guided hunts. It wasn't ideal, but it was an option.

"Don't get your hopes up," the officer replied when Bill told her the news. "If he's deemed a vicious dog, you legally can't give him away."

Ann didn't understand who this woman was, or why she was trying to lasso Duke with a long pole.

"So, what happens then?" Daniel asked.

"You have two choices: put him down or build him a pen at least twelve feet high to keep him in at all times."

"But the Cordillera Homeowners Association won't allow a fence that high," Bill said.

"Sir, I'm just telling you the law."

"It's an Obamanation if you ask me," Ann said, standing beside her husband as the officer loaded the dog into the cage.

"Excuse me?"

"Nothing," Daniel said. "What about the dog? What do you think his chances are?"

"Honestly?" the woman said, looking directly at Ann. "With his record, I'm going to recommend he be put down."

Three days later, the Greenwoods received two pieces of bad news concerning the dog. First, they received a letter explaining that they had been dropped from their homeowner and umbrella policies after the insurance company chose to settle with the satellite guy for fourteen thousand dollars. Then, later in the afternoon, they received a call from the county. Ann could tell from the expression on her husband's face that the news wasn't good.

"Can we at least say goodbye?" Bill asked.

Ann wondered who was leaving.

***

When Ann entered the room with Bill, Duke jumped to his feet, eager for his release and to get back home. Ann thought he must've missed Lizzie and running the perimeter. Her husband approached the metal cage and began playing with the dog's ears and touching his nose and big front paws. It was a side of Bill that few had ever seen. It reminded Ann of a puppy they'd owned decades ago. What was his name? Hondo? A sweet yellow Lab pup with ears too big for his body, Hondo rode home on Ann's lap all the way back to the house on Patchester. This Ann remembered very clearly.

"I'm sorry, partner." Bill knelt in front of the cage. "I did all I could do, but you won't feel a thing. I promise. I'm sorry we let you down, buddy."

With some difficulty, Bill got back to his feet, turned, and hugged Ann. He squeezed her tight. She felt his chest heaving as he sobbed on her shoulder. She patted him on the back in the same way she used to with the children when they skinned their knees. With a snort and a clearing of his throat, Bill pulled away and took Ann by the wrist, wiping the tears from his face, and walked out the door.

Looking over her shoulder as she was pulled from the room, Ann stole one last look at the dog. She could tell that he didn't understand any more than she did.

***

It took several days for Bill and Ann to return their son's phone call. Bill knew what it was about and wasn't ready to talk yet. At least, that's what he told Ann when he waved her away from the call.

Finally, Bill made himself a scotch and sat with the phone at the breakfast room table. Ann sat across from him with the other portable phone. When he finished his drink, Bill made the call.

"I guess you know by now."

"I heard. How are y'all doing?"

"Better than Duke."

"It's a shame," Ann added.

"I've been reading Caesar's book," Bill said. "There's an entire chapter called 'How We Screw Up Our Dogs,' and I'm guilty of most of it."

"You can't beat yourself up, Dad. You need to move on. Have you thought about getting another dog? Maybe a lab—they're good family dogs."

"They're no good for quail," Bill said.

"But you're not hunting quail. That's the problem."

"But I might."

Ann watched and listened.

"You always said that your labs were the best hunters you'd ever had. And remember how good Hondo was when Sara and I were little."

Bill got up and went to fix another drink.

"He was a good dog," Ann said.

"I hunted ducks and geese back then. It's different."

"Do you think you have that many hunts left?"

"I'd like to think I do," Bill said as he returned to the table.

Daniel continued to press. "Remember that time when we were sitting in that duck blind flicking icicles off Hondo's muzzle, and he didn't even shiver? That dog was a soldier."

"Yeah, he was a good one."

"He was a good one," Ann said.

"What about the time we were dove hunting in Katy with your buddy that kept claiming everything that fell out of the sky."

"Roy Fox."

"I remember him. He was the Australian, right?"

"No, dear," Ann said. "That's Forney you're thinking of."

There was a long silence on the line. Bill looked at Ann—puzzled.

"Remember how Hondo snatched that bird right out of the air, and you asked Fox if he'd hit that one, too."

"That bastard said he thought he clipped one earlier in the day."

They all laughed.

When the laughter subsided and Daniel started into his next story, Ann noticed something wasn't right. She looked around the room several times, and then she said it.

"Where's Duke?"

Another silence followed.

"Duke is dead, dear. Remember?"

"Oh, right. I'm sorry. I'm just so used to him being around. It's a shame, isn't it?"

"It is."

Ann knotted her hands and clinched her fists beneath the table, silently repeating to herself: *Duke is dead, dear. Duke is dead, dear. Duke is dead, dear...* until she was sure it was committed to memory.

About the Author

Doug S. Haines is a Texas-born musician and writer. In 2013, he co-authored *Resurrecting Trash*, a book about sustainable living published by Texas Review Press. His fiction has appeared in journals such as *Slippery Elm, Reed Magazine*, and *The Chicago Tribune's Printers Row.* He teaches English and writing at Sam Houston State University in Huntsville, TX, where he lives with his wife, Katie, and their two dogs, Lucille and Mabel.

About the Press

Unsolicited Press is a Pacific Northwest publishing house that puts authors first and paychecks last. Our editors are volunteers working across the country to see beautiful books come to life. For more information on Unsolicited Press, visit www.unsolicitedpress.com

www.ingramcontent.com/pod-product-compliance
Lightning Source LLC
Chambersburg PA
CBHW032004180726
48283CB00008B/2561

* 9 7 8 1 9 4 7 0 2 1 1 9 8 *